Fall From Grace

Fall From Grace

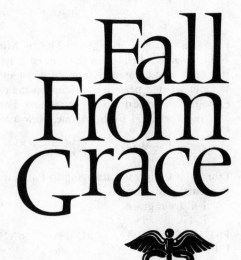

MIRIAM
BORGENICHT

ST. MARTIN'S PRESS
New York

Design by Lee Wade

Library of Congress Cataloging in Publication Data
Borgenicht, Miriam.
     Fall from grace.
     I. Title.
PS3552.O75F3 1984   813'.54   83-24660
ISBN 0-312-27978-7

First Edition
10 9 8 7 6 5 4 3 2 1

Fall
From
Grace

Chapter
ONE

THOSE WHO HELD NAN DUNLOP RESPONSIBLE for William Gardiner's death said afterwards that she had been the one to do the courting. She had schemed and maneuvered and connived so he would notice her. Well, Nan thought, it was perfectly true. It had to be true. How could he know of her existence unless she conducted an operation of great stealth and tenacity? A doctor, a distinguished doctor, doesn't notice a nurse; she doesn't impinge on his consciousness any more than the aide who walks ahead of him pushing the food tray or the therapist who scuttles out of a patient's room when he marches in with his entourage. Of necessity, stealth and tenaciousness defined her. Girl gets Boy: Let Boy be a celebrated lung specialist at one of New York's great hospitals and Girl a registered nurse, and the strategy is still the same. Gotham General Hospital was her hunting ground: every crowded elevator a haven where she could with impunity press close to him, every nurse's station a trysting place where she was the one to hand him the charts, every antiseptic corridor a lover's lane on which she accompanied Dr. William Gardiner on his rounds.

They also said, however, those envious or mean-spirited people who had it in for her, that she did it for money, and that was not true. She fell in love. Though even her dearest friend found it hard to credit, she fell deeply, irreversibly, in love. Oh, she knew perfectly well that every mandate of myth and logic decreed otherwise. Young girl gets sugar daddy: right out of everyone's most profound beliefs. An absolute. But the facts did not conform. She heard him say, "When the nodule grows larger, the tissue cells at its center may degenerate and decompose," and she was gone. It broke her up. "Oh, God, his voice," she whispered to Rosanne, whom she'd cajoled into coming with her. In the back of the room where William was lecturing to the medical students, she stood rapt in her nylon uniform: a woman in love.

Well, love. Another concept to make the cynical eyebrows rise. Her friends were ready with the theories to explain why a twenty-six-year-old girl goes soft in the head over a sixty-seven-year-old man. She's looking to replace the father who abandoned her. She's looking to replace the father who did not abandon her. She didn't complete the Oedipal transfer. She's making up for what she missed at eight or eleven or fourteen. Okay, okay, Nan thought; if that kind of glib pedantry makes it more palatable to them, let them have it. What she didn't tell them, what didn't seem remotely necessary for them to hear, was that far from regarding William in paternal terms, she pictured him the way a woman pictures any man she falls for— making love to her.

It was also unnecessary to confide another truth, which was that the paternal aspect was wholly absent from his lovemaking. She knew, of course, she was not his first. The hospital grapevine is among the more hardy of indoor plants, and she was never in any doubt about the succession of nurses, women doctors, lab assistants, hospital administrators who preceded her. But I'm the one he married, she contentedly thought. I was the one to convince him it would be good to settle down. And the settling suited him. Astonished joy. She supposed some men were dependent on an element of furtiveness for that extra fillip of pleasure, but not, it turned out, William. Substituting candor for circumspection simply made things better. Newly embarked on a course in which one woman and one only was to be on hand, he clearly was finding within himself new aptitudes for passion.

She was the one only, and on a Sunday morning in October Nan Dunlop and William Gardiner were married, and on Sunday afternoon they ran an open house in his apartment on the twenty-third floor of the splendid building, two blocks from the hospital, where they were going to live. An event? William didn't think so. No one much will come, was what he said.

She knew better than to argue. But she also knew the prurient curiosity that along with bemused good will was inevitable for a match like theirs, and she had a little talk with the caterer. She was right. A bash. They all came, all of them with their assessing gaze. Drs. Calvano and Paul and Brinkworth from William's staff, and the medical director of the hospital, and its entire public relations staff, and Ben Davis of orthopedics, who was William's dear friend, and two women doctors with whom William had had affairs, and Rosanne and her young man Steve who sold surgical supplies, and a Dr. Tad Collins who'd trained under William twenty-one years earlier and was just that week up from Washington, where he practiced, and six nurses from West 9, which had been her floor before she contrived to move to East 9 in her siege of William, and more. Many more. Everyone except Aunt Martha, who was her only relative and who sent word about the heart murmur that just might be activated if she took the trip.

They all came and drank champagne and kissed the bride and drank more champagne and offered tipsy congratulations. And William loved it. In the bleak days that came after, she used to remind herself how much he loved that party. His big exuberant head pushed through the crowd, kissing all the proffered cheeks and mouths, and calling responses across the amiable pandemonium, and meeting with unapologetic smiles the urbane bafflement of the women who hadn't been the ones to nab him. And making clear his delight with his new acquisition. Me, she thought. Nan Dunlop, R.N.

That was Sunday, and on Wednesday the honeymoon was to start, and on Monday he said would she come with him to his lawyer's?

"William, dear, whatever for?"

"Keep me company while I sign my will."

"What a time to sign a will when we have all that—"

"Shopping. I know. Your raincoat. My slacks. But new wills have to be signed."

"I don't get it."

"I have a wife, so she's the one to inherit my estate rather than the Institute for Applied Pulmonary Studies in case anything—Angel, don't look so grim. I have no intention of dying. Wills are just something to be got through."

She shook her head. He had it wrong. Wills didn't represent to her an embodiment of menace. She'd been around too many death scenes, had in a sense officiated at them; she knew how bad they were, and how much worse if the appropriate legal dispensations were not in place.

She turned from the window. Her own studio apartment had looked out on a wall ten feet distant; his was allotted a sweep of river and city. "Okay, a new will, I suppose you have to. But do it someday. Six months from now. A year."

He laughed. He hugged her. He said they didn't wait to get married and now he didn't see why they should wait for this customary observance of the married state.

Actually, she thought, he doesn't see, any more than he saw why the prurient would flock to their party. That was

William; there were certain small-minded scruples that his vision didn't accommodate. Well, suppose she enlightened him? William, dear, look at it this way. Here's someone young and poor marrying someone elderly and rich. If she also makes a mint in the process, don't you see there might be some, well, indelicacy? Or that people might deduce some indelicacy?

No, she couldn't tell him. Couldn't lay that sordid picture before his serene pleasure. Besides, he said it was already done, the new will ordered and discussed and written, and he wanted her to come tomorrow when he signed it.

Back where they had been. "I should come to your lawyer's?"

"Just a formality. Take a second."

"If it's a second, why should I come?"

"I want you to meet him."

"This lawyer—what's his name? Victor?"

"Victor Hemmings."

"Do you mean you want him to meet me?"

"That too," William said nicely.

"If our meeting is so important, why didn't he come to the party?"

"He wished he could. He had weekend plans with his son."

She looked up quickly, but there was only the easy expression in the deep blue eyes. "He didn't want you to change your will, did he?" she said.

"You know lawyers. Trained in wariness."

"He was against your marrying me altogether."

"He won't be when he meets you," William answered.

She looked at him, at that large, wonderful, equable face. All right, I'll go with him even though I don't think it's a good idea, in fact, it's a rotten idea, going to witness the signing of a will that makes me the beneficiary, and besides I don't think Victor will make it easy, but William wants it and anything William wants.

Victor didn't make it easy. Oh, he was very civil, that practiced civility washing over her as he came out to greet them in the reception room and took them into his office and offered celebratory drinks and said all the right things. How good to meet her and he'd been hearing and he could kick himself that he had this long-time plan for a weekend trip with his son. He even showed the son's picture. An eight- or nine-year-old with his father's heavy eyebrows and long, thin, nice-looking face.

She said the right things too. Cute. Sensitive. Full of more energy than they know what to do with.

Victor put the picture back on his desk. "William saved his life, you know."

She did know. It was one of those classic medical sagas in which luck and genius—telling her, William had of course stressed the former—play an equal part. The two men, William with whoever had been his current lady friend and Victor with the son he was bringing up alone, having summer cottages on the same block, and a child's sudden high fever, and a soothing dismissal, let's wait and see, from the doctor called in first, and an hour later a frantic plea to Dr. Gardiner three doors away.

She knew and said so, but Victor's voice went on anyhow. ". . . said do nothing, these fevers in summer, and then the convulsions and I called William, I didn't even know him, we'd just nodded on the beach, and he came, on a beautiful Sunday afternoon he came over to an absolute stranger's, and he took one look and said get moving, and they said at the hospital that if another half hour . . ."

She sat quietly. It was obvious why he was going through it. His way of saying there's a bond; we're not just lawyer and client; we're buddies, and don't you forget it. William saved his child, which instilled in William's heart an ineradicable warmth, and now Victor was serving notice that he was prepared to perform a similar function should it be needed. Victor the savior.

He was smart enough, too, to cut it short and shift to something else, like where were they going on their honeymoon? Good question. While William embarked with cheerful thoroughness on the plans, she felt Victor appraise her. Too pretty. Curly hair. Even features. Good figure . . . his eyes ticking off the incontrovertible assets.

"And then back first week in November. Three weeks on the button."

Victor said it sounded great.

"Honeymoon of the year." William took her hand.

"Lloyd Prentice came back from Amsterdam last week," Victor said.

Lloyd? Lloyd was in the office? A small meditative pause. Then William stood. "I should say hello to him. Angel, be right back."

She nodded. Typical. William figured that her charms would go over bigger, erase any residual reluctance, if she and Victor were alone for a little while.

And for a second the idea exercised its seductive power over her too. After all, this civilized office, with the leather volumes and the walnut paneling and the engravings and, faintly, through the open door, the click of the typewriter of the conscientious-looking secretary in the alcove outside —all that paraphernalia to connote fairness, justice—how could he not like her? How could malevolent thoughts exist in this gilt-edged air?

That delusive comfort went on for a second. Then she was conscious of Victor's face leaning at her across the desk.

"Look here. I love that man. Really love him, do you

hear? You may think he's just a good-time Charlie, but not so. There are depths. Rare and complicated aspects. And I don't want him hurt. I won't allow any injury to his spirit. Do you know what I'm getting at? Yes, I think you do. Mrs. Gardiner, I think we understand each other perfectly."

Well, there were plenty of answers. Proud outrage. Contemptuous fury. Even unabashed candor—yes, best of all, maybe, unabashed candor: Oh, God, if you only knew how I'm the one who loves him. The unspoken words rang in her ears, a great, defiant, bellicose outburst. And all so obvious—incredible that they didn't come pouring out of their own volition. All the self-evident truths to make him cringe.

But it was his office. His timing. Most of all, his aura of unassailable success, and she stood silent—it occurred to her that she must look as guilty as he thought her. Oh, what he was saying was no worse than some people were thinking, as she reminded herself in her bad moments, but it took her breath away to be regarded with such rancor. She felt weak. She wanted to throw up. She walked over to the window, and that's how they were, that uninformative tableau, she with her dazed stare fixed on the midtown towers outside and Victor fastidiously assembling papers, when William came back.

It went fast after that. Strictly business. Victor pulled out some long sheets and said, "Here it is. Just what you ordered. A will making your wife the sole beneficiary."

"And making you executor, you put that in too, didn't you?"

Did he tell Nan about that? Victor asked.

He told her now. "Angel, nothing's going to happen to me, but if it should, you'll be in good hands. The most able lawyer in New York taking care of your affairs. You're lucky, we're both damn lucky to have him."

She sat stiffly, her back not touching the chair. If she looked up, met Victor's eyes, would there be a message in them? She didn't look up, didn't say anything—for a second there was only the sound of that conscientious typing outside. Then William said, "Where do I sign?" and Victor said, "Don't you want to read it?" and William said, "You read it, that's enough," and with two lawyers from next door looking on as witnesses, he bent over and affixed his name. Done and done. Nan Dunlop Gardiner the beneficiary of William's estate and Victor Hemmings her executor.

Then the festive note started again. Lloyd Prentice and two other partners came in because word had obviously spread that here was a chance to meet Dr. Gardiner's cute young wife, and the assiduous secretary found a reason to bring papers into the office, and Victor got out more glasses, and it was a party. A going-away party, everyone imbued with the conviction that his particular advice is going to make the difference. Going to Europe, you two? Oh, then you must stay at. Be sure to get to. Don't forget to look up.

And Victor participated. Or if he didn't, there was enough cordiality in his manner so no one noticed. And the moment was lost. Though by then the defense had formed clearly in her mind, there was no time when she was alone with Victor to hurl it. And she didn't tell William. Going down in the elevator, she saw no way that she could tell William; after all that jolly helpfulness it would have sounded unreal, and the next two days produced no occasion for it, and by then they were on the honeymoon of the year, and for her too Victor's words took on the aspect of unreality. She, Nan, injure William's spirit! Hurt him in any way! Even fail to appreciate him! Ludicrous. Surely that astounding accusation had not been made, she had never heard it.

Chapter
TWO

THEY STAYED AT ALL THE RIGHT PLACES and got to the recommended sights and looked up the appropriate contacts, and it was fine. That is, it was fine because of William's being the kind of person he was. After a couple of days, she realized there was no use pretending that if a sixty-seven-year-old man and a twenty-six-year-old woman travel together, they can melt into the background. And in their case, the difference was intensified because of the way they wore their age. William's commanding bulk and picturesque features connoted dignity, which to some minds connotes age; in bearing and manner he could pass for fifty, but a cursory look might put him down as seventy-five. As for her, there was something about her wayward hair and even features that made her look younger than she was—she couldn't count the times she'd gone into a room and started to adjust the IV, to have the patient say, "Are you sure you know how to do it, dear?" And if you're a mismatched couple—oh, it's true—you get the eye. Even the hotel clerk allows himself an amazed blink before putting on his face of courteous disinterest; as for those standing around, you can see them go the route from amused skepticism to interested surmise. Once, after William wrote "Dr. and Mrs. Gardiner" in his large undoctorlike script, she heard a woman say, "Mrs. Gardiner, my foot," before they had even left the desk. And another time the porter who took them to their room hesitated. Hesitated why? Tip given and all—what's he after? Finally he came out with it: They could have single beds; the management provided them. She was furious. What did he think, this young snip who lugged suitcases? Madam wanted to sneak out at midnight to meet her young lover? The strain of lovemaking would leave the gentleman needing a bed of his own?

She was furious, but William laughed. He laughed at all the inquisitive, pushy, misguided speculation. He laughed right through the three weeks, and presently, becoming as inured as he was, she laughed delightedly with him. Curious. She fell in love with the thoughtful, concerned, intelligent man at the hospital, but this other man must have been there too, this one capable of such vast enjoyment; some intuition must have revealed him to her. And wasn't this another sign that they were right for each other, that all must go well with them?

And actually, once they were home, things continued well for several weeks. Oh, they did, they did; when she looked back, she honestly thought so. William returned to his practice, and without missing a beat, she went back to her job. Back where she belonged. West 9. She wanted to. For one thing, she liked being a nurse. Okay, not all of it: measuring I and O, suctioning, holding a basin while someone vomits—any nurse who doesn't mind it, find out what she's hiding, she and Rosanne always said. But you like what you do well, and as nurses go, she knew she was up there with the best.

And for another thing, she wanted to avoid any appearance of having profited from marriage. Did that indicate a weakness in her character, that obsessed concern with what others thought? People who wrote great books or made brilliant discoveries were surely above such small-minded fears; she envisioned them, those superior creatures, as suspended in an imperial self-sufficiency wherein, dogged, detached, they churned out their memorable achievements. But she'd never cared to write a great book or make a brilliant discovery; what she wanted, what she ardently had to have, was people's good opinion. In a way, she supposed it contributed to her excellence as a nurse. That is, if the patient in 908a was slated for a mastectomy, Nan Dunlop was the one in there before she went down. "Marge, I know you're scared, but it might be just a fibro-cystitis; believe me, I've seen it plenty of times. And even if not . . ." Emotional caring was the heavy-handed term, and of course it was important that Marge be in an easier frame of mind as they trundled her off. But what also mattered was that they admire her, Nan Dunlop; as Marge clutched her hand, she would be thinking that after the operation the groggy voice would say, "That cute nurse with the curly hair, she's the one I want."

Anyhow, this was her world—Amy Harkness, the supervisor, and Bea Spiro, the head nurse, and the other RN's on the floor, and Mrs. Jefferson the practical nurse who always backed her up, and Doctors Rosen and Belair, who depended on her for all kinds of unacknowledged helpfulness —all the people waiting, as she saw it, to find out the score. Did she marry him just for the cash? Now she's in the chips, will she take it easy? Rosanne made clear what route she herself would take. "Honestly, Nan, I don't figure it. If it was me, that kind of windfall, you wouldn't catch me slaving my butt off another second." Well, Rosanne wasn't saddled with her kind of sensitivity; Rosanne would not, for instance, have kept Victor in mind. It wasn't true that his words were unreal; there he was, the rancorous face and cruel imputation coming at her across his desk, making her push herself even harder. She was not just back on the job, she was back on the job with religious scrupulosity. One morning when she had the kind of sore throat that gives anyone sanction for a day in bed, she dragged herself up and dosed herself with pills and was in the nurse's station for Report at seven. Nan, the model nurse. Everything the same.

Except things are never the same. Okay, there were no indulgences on the floor—no nurse could be indulged on West 9—but when she walked down the halls or waited for the elevator or stood on line in the cafeteria, she was Dr. Gardiner's wife. There was that. Indisputable. Doctors who usually looked past her offered an elaborate hello. Sometimes they stopped for a few words. Sometimes they ate with her. And the one who ate with her most was Tad Collins.

At first she didn't even know who he was, this man with the sandy hair and round, friendly face standing next to her as she started on her tuna-fish sandwich.

"You don't remember me."

"Nope."

"I trained under William twenty-one—oh, lord, twenty-two years ago."

"Oh, yes. You came to the party."

"You throw a great party."

"That party threw itself," she said honestly. Then she said William had wondered how he knew about their being married.

From Tad, a nice smile. "Did he? Did he really? That's William. Modest. When if he'd be realistic he'd know no one could be in a hospital five minutes last month without hearing the big news about Dr. Gardiner—listen, mind if I sit down?"

She surely didn't mind if he was going to keep talking about William. About his modesty, which actually wasn't

all that great, and also about his brilliance, which was.
Especially about these attributes from the standpoint of
one who had seen them at first hand during his own years
of training. But as it turned out, what they mostly talked
about was her. No, they talked about nursing; even better.
How did they get there? She wasn't sure; she certainly
didn't complain about her lot, but there it was, she with her
sandwich, Tad with some soup and a salad, while he gave
a little discourse coinciding with every nurse's private
creed.

"Nurse and doctor, no profession has anything quite like
it. That particular relationship, I mean. Take lawyers. A
lawyer has a young lawyer to do his dirty work. The grubbing to get one footnote, turn up a single obscure case. But
the young lawyers will get to be old lawyers some day.
Successful. Distinguished. Or at least they'll have a crack
at it. They're in the running. On the same track as those
they work for. But the ones who do the doctors' dirty work
will never be professional equals. They'll always be an
insurmountable rung below. Outside the pale in the only
hierarchy that counts. Second-class citizens.

"Am I keeping you? Do you have to run? Second-class
citizens—right. Just what we've made of them. Don't get
me wrong, there's been improvement. Ask William. I bet
he remembers a time when nurses had to give doctors their
chairs when those estimable gods came into a room. They
don't expect that kind of subservience today. But they also
don't use what nurses could give, which is an enormous
store of intuitive understanding. Did I say 'they'? Me. I'm
as high-handed as the next one. I had a patient before I left.
Mechanized edema—do I operate or not? Well, part of the
decision is purely medical, of course, but part is something
else. What kind of care will she get from her family? What's
her frame of mind? Is she in there fighting? These ought to

be factored into the picture too. So do I call on the judgment of the person in the best position to know all this? Do I say, Emmy Lou, you've been taking care of that woman for a month, come to staff meeting today and give us your thoughts? Not on your life. It's my show. My ego trip. Listen, eat your sandwich."

She didn't have to eat. His words warmed her, sustained her. They were what every nurse yearned to hear: You're unappreciated, you don't get credit for all your skilled and onerous work. And here she was hearing it not from another nurse at one of those gripe sessions they all treated themselves to once in a while, but from the person they most want the appreciation from, which is a doctor. Oh, he intended to please, she could see that perfectly well; sitting at the long table, with three interns exchanging notes at the other end and a kitchen boy clattering dishes beside them, he was definitely a man exercising his charm. But he was also speaking his mind, he must be; could his words ring with such earnest plausibility if he weren't?

She didn't ask William if he remembered a time when nurses stood up to give doctors their chair, but she did ask him about Tad. Yes. Knew him well. Or twenty-some years ago knew him well. Bright. Able. A distinguished doctor. Had stayed in Washington all these years, but was doing some work on bronchial cancer, which was why he was here for a few weeks. Married some years ago but perhaps not now—maybe she would find out.

Not married—she did find out. It was one of the few personal items they discussed. Mainly their talk proceeded along the lines of their first meeting, as she told Rosanne.

"He has some very interesting ideas about nursing."

"Hmm." Such a pretty girl, Rosanne, with red hair and the requisite pale skin and pointed features, which she turned thoughtfully at Nan's words. They were in the nurses' lounge on their morning break. "Is that what he told you about on Wednesday? And the time before that when you were off at that corner table?"

Nan nodded. It was true that Tad Collins turned up a lot: at the east door when she got off work, in hallways, on the stairs she took at lunchtime. It didn't fool her; who knew better than she that a hospital wasn't the place for easy timing? You say meet me in front of the elevator at twelve, but the senile patient in 922 falls out of her wheelchair, or the new nurse says help me lift this man, or the post-op case goes into respiratory shock just as you're walking down the hall. So she knew, she should know, that anyone who turned up casually had waited designedly. She didn't mind. All right, be honest; she liked it. It was part of her expansive new life: the ecstatic nights with William, and the apartment that ran without her lifting a finger, and at lunch an old colleague of her husband's who obviously found her attractive.

"He might do an article about the nurse's role in treatment decisions," she said.

Another caustic look from the pointed features. "I'm beat," Rosanne said. "Steve and I heard of this apartment, supposed to be cheap, so we went out last night after supper. Cheap! Well! You have to put twenty thousand down, and maintenance is over three hundred, so even if forty percent is deductible there's that bite, and then you have to figure what you lose in interest by closing out your savings, and then of course the extra subway. And we didn't even like it all that much. I mean, if that's the story, we can wait; I'll stay where I am, thanks."

I get it, Nan thought. Get what's behind this catalogue of dissatisfaction. She's too nice, Rosanne is, to criticize directly, but what she's really saying is here I am with my unsuccessful man and my postponed marriage and my skimpy options, and there you are with that sensational husband and a glamorous apartment that overlooks half the city, and servants, and money, and you still have to latch on to the first newly available man—honestly, it isn't fair. No malice in Rosanne's voice, just that simple attribution of unfairness, but Nan saw the point. Tad and she had indeed been a conspicuous twosome. Too conspicuous—unnecessary. Hereafter she'd start using different routes and shift into different schedules. Nothing overt. Just a hint.

And it would have worked. Tad would have taken the hint, and it would have ended. It was William who kept things going.

Chapter
THREE

WHAT HAPPENED WAS THAT when she came home one afternoon he said he had gout and couldn't go to the testimonial dinner for Ben Davis that night and she should go with Tad.

She sat next to him on the couch. William with gout! With any disease that signals the diminution that is a concomitant of age. And why was he telling her in this abrupt, this really harsh manner when she'd burst in full of expectation of the evening they were going to spend together? She didn't know he had gout, was what she finally said.

"I have a tendency to it. Sometimes the tendency kicks up."

"Can't you take something?"

"I did. I called Bill Leroy and he sent down some Zyloprim. Takes time to work. I still don't feel right."

He didn't look right. It was nothing she could specifically point to: simply that the aura of assured heartiness that his big face usually gave off was somehow missing. She took his hand. "William, you'll be better."

"Sure. Tomorrow." From that altered face, a beatific smile.

"So we'll stay home. We'll listen to—"

"I can't insult Ben Davis. His big evening—if I'm not there, at least my wife has to be."

"We'll tell him you have—"

"Angel, you don't understand. A dinner for Ben—he'd never forgive me. But if you're there, you and Tad . . ."

That was when it registered. "I should go with Tad Collins!"

"I wouldn't want you to go alone."

She heard the ineffectual sputter of her own voice: "But if . . . we don't . . . but I . . ." Finally she said, "Friday night, Tad probably has a million things."

"No. He's free. He'd be glad."

"You asked him to take me!"

"Angel, it was a crisis."

She stood up. Impossible—why didn't he realize? Sending your pretty young wife to a public dinner with another man—it was asking for trouble. Even if you had every reason to feel sure of her devotion, it was a perverse kind of asking for trouble.

On the other hand, how could she say so? It would be like one of those self-fulfilling prophecies: The financial wiz says stocks will go down, and by God they do go down:

public confidence shattered. In the same way, William's confidence might just be shattered if she suggested there were reasons why Tad and she shouldn't appear together in front of all his friends and colleagues; doubts might brush against that warm loving confident mind; he might see things that didn't exist.

"William, what's the matter?" That abstracted look on his face.

"Nothing. You reminded me of someone I knew long ago. It's nothing. Wear your velvet suit to the dinner."

"William, I won't—it's out of the question—don't ask me again—just the most ridiculous—I absolutely—"

He was very sweet. Held her till she stopped crying and sat with her while she dressed and then, like the pictorially correct husband of the advertisements, came over to clasp her necklace. Then, for a second, panic. Will he also be around to hand her over to Tad? Another pictorial vignette: Now see you take good care of my little girl, young man. But that much sensitivity he had. "Tell Tad I'm sorry I can't see him," William said as he went to bed a few minutes before the doorbell rang.

What she told Tad was more fatuous. Remarks like I hope you don't mind, and Ben Davis and William having been such good friends, and William really appreciates. He took the measure of her unease; though his round face maintained its expression of friendly concern, he didn't talk much; even when they were seated at one of those grandiose tables for ten that are a staple of public dinners, he didn't talk much, which she thought showed a discerning consideration. Leave it to Tad to reserve his enthusiastic comments for whoever was on his other side, which left her free to talk to the doctor on her left, which helped efface the fact that William Gardiner's wife and Tad Collins were here as a couple.

Well, everyone knows what those testimonial dinners are. The sluggish jokes, the forced laughter, the stale camaraderie of men who have been joined in the same hierarchical struggles, the same punishing need to stay on top. Plus, of course, the adulatory testimony to one who did his big work maybe fifteen years before and receives the homage with a stilted smile. After the speeches they cluster around him, as they do around an aging movie star, but interest has waned; they look someplace else.

They looked at her. She was the novelty. Nan Dunlop Gardiner, with her wayward hair and rosy face and cute figure in a brown velvet suit. Ben Davis might receive the praise, but she was the celebrity. Someone fresh, pretty, sexy among the discreetly censorious wives. Oh, you know, that little nurse William Gardiner married. . . . No, I never thought he would either.

There was sedate dancing after the speeches, and she was the one they danced with. The nurse who used to be treated to patronizing neglect while Drs. Ashton and Byer and Pecora discussed her patient was wafted from Dr. Ashton's arms to Dr. Byer's and then—Hey, my turn—to Dr. Pecora's. Same face, but they saw it differently. She was William's wife and Tad's date and flushed too, she was aware, with the consciousness of her own desirability.

Oh, she knew she should leave. Having sat at prim attention through the speeches and gone up with her own proper handshake, she should walk out. A demure exit. Dinner, yes; dancing, no—she knew perfectly well. But she also knew the sensation of being sought after, that gaudy triumph. Belle of the ball. Nothing like it since she was sixteen.

Tad was the one to remind her it was time to leave: Tad whose solicitude reached new heights on the way home. Because he didn't make a pass. Not even an avuncular arm around her bedraggled shoulder. Had William been a younger man, she figured, there would have been something after all that dancing and flitting. A casual kiss, at the very least. A whispered proposition, the more sweetly voluptuous in that both parties would know it had no chance. As it was, he sat stilted on his side of the taxi, the round face and sandy hair set straight ahead as though posing for some archaic photograph. That exercise in ostentatious control —in a way it's more sexy than the alternative. It establishes a presence, so though you make the obligatory remarks— nice party, so good for Ben Davis, oh, yes, wonderful doctor—through all the mechanical talk, you think, dear God, he's really holding himself in. The taxi reeks with the excitement of repressed torment.

And it has an effect. It releases something, some erotic air, just as the real thing would. It was with the sense of denied sexuality that she got out of the taxi, and after all his punctilious behavior let Tad hold her hand as they went into the lobby, and he was still holding it when they met Victor Hemmings getting out of the elevator.

"Oh. Goodness. Hello. I didn't know you were . . . Well, I don't think you know Dr. Collins."

A respite, while she performed the introductions and Tad extended to Victor the hand that had been clasped to hers. But a handshake leads inexorably to nothing, and standing in that unhelpful lobby she felt constrained to keep things going. "Tad trained under William long ago. They, um, worked together."

Still no natural sequitur, none at least that either of them was moved to provide. All right, it was on her. "You've been visiting William?"

"Certainly have."

"How'd you find him?" she asked with grim brightness.

"Moderately miserable. That is, he sounded miserable on

the phone so I thought I'd come." His clipped voice
stopped short as if to let her reconstruct the conversation.
Well, it lent itself to reconstruction, all right: "You say
you're sick?" "Just a touch of gout." "And all alone?" "Nan
went to this dinner." "Ah." "One of us had to be there."
"I see." "I wanted her to go." Another knowing "Ah."

Continued silence. Victor was wearing a green tur-
tleneck and slacks—the hardworking lawyer's fatigue
outfit—but it emphasized the festive look that emanated
from Tad and her. She could see him studying her again—
flushed cheeks, open jacket, disarrayed hair—and his face
twisted so that for a second she thought he might actually
raise a hand and hit her. But a gray-haired couple came in
and rang for the elevator, and under their neighborly stare
the men did finally make a stab at talking. Tad said, these
dinners, so rewarding for someone like Ben Davis, really
serve a purpose, and Victor said lawyers had them too, a
bore but necessary; oh, yes, he agreed.

She took a breath. "It was nice of you to come."

"I was damn glad to have the chance."

"I know William liked having you."

"Yes, he seemed to want company," Victor said.

Okay, okay. "I really appreciate it."

"Oh, I did it for William," Victor said as the elevator
door opened and she and Tad could get in at last.

Tad waited till the other couple got off. "Now who is
that man?"

"He's William's lawyer. He idolizes William. Well, it's
mutual, I guess."

"Is he always so hostile?"

"You noticed it then?"

"He sure as hell didn't try to hide it."

When they got off at their floor she could see them in the
vestibule mirror: a girl in a velvet suit biting her lower lip

as she takes the key out of her bag, a man looking down at her with an expression of puzzled concern.

"He didn't want William to marry me, he thinks . . . he thinks I married William for his money," she burst out.

"Oh, my dear, my sweet Nan. People are rotten, aren't they?"

She was the one to kiss him then. She reached up, and planted a quick kiss on his surprised cheek, and squeezed his hand, and went in fast, because this evening had gone on long enough.

Chapter
FOUR

TAD WAS WRONG. People weren't rotten; no, she would never believe that. But they surely were observant; especially if you had all the luck, they made of observation a high art, and she realized again what a mistake it had been to stay at that dinner. What did she think she was doing, acting like a lordly adolescent while the wives cast at her those splinter glances of envious rectitude? Besides, she hadn't even liked the dancing—those doctors with their pedantic little steps stored up from twenty, thirty years before. So different from William, whose large body moved beautifully on the dance floor while his feet seemed automatically to appropriate whatever was new and graceful.

Besides, these days he seemed—not unwell, that was over by the next day, but tense. More and more she saw on his face the abstracted look he had worn when he sent her to that dinner. As if he were looking through her, past her. And asking if he was all right did no good. "Oh, sure, Angel, fine," but he wasn't fine. He broke off conversations in the middle. He left his food. He sat without turning the page of his book. Once she asked another question. "Who do I remind you of? Remember you said—"

"It was long ago."

"That resemblance, is it something you—"

"Angel, don't worry."

Well, of course she worried. If a man changed so the spirit seemed to go out of him, why wouldn't his wife worry? And one morning she asked why he didn't sleep the night before.

She asked without any great hope of a breakthrough, and none was available. Did he not sleep? Not last night, not the two or three nights before? Well, maybe not. Life, he vaguely said.

"Is it because . . . William, listen. Has it anything to do, I mean, is it related to our being married?"

End of vagueness. "Ah, my sweet idiot, my dearest Nan. Wash your mouth out. Never say anything like that again."

Still no progress. Once, after everything was settled between them, she'd asked him why he never got married before. The time wasn't propitious, he said, which of course was no answer at all. Now she thought maybe it's never propitious. Doctor-nurse: the truth is, not everyone is in favor. Oh, it fulfills some misty expectations about the romantic drama of hospital life, but ask the hospital administrators, ask the other doctors, their faces tell a different story. A doctor-nurse match is threatening; like miscegenation, it cuts across sacrosanct lines, engenders laxness, encourages the wrong ideas. Elderly doctor, young nurse—even worse; it impairs discipline in that society most dependent on a strict adherence to the hierarchical values.

Was that it, then—he was responding to the subtle nuances of disapprobation? Subtle nuances! Her William! Oh, she knew better than that.

All right, some minor problem. "William, if it goes on another night, take a pill. Just till—What goes on here! Me prescribing to the doctor."

"Feel free, Angel."

"Well, one pill, to break it up. We have them, don't we? No? Then bring some home."

"Okay." Abstracted again.

"You'll forget. Listen. Write me a prescription, I'll pick it up for you at the hospital."

He kissed her, and she thought, maybe she'd been lax too. She'd be more aggressive about planning diversions, taking him out, providing the circumstances in which he could have fun. So it was providential when she had a bona fide reason to call him that afternoon and ask him to come home early.

"William? William, dear, the phone was ringing when I walked into the house, and guess who? Aunt Martha. Oh, not her, of course, Celia, the woman who takes care of her. Aunt Martha had one of her attacks, and Celia says the doctor is making something of it, and they want me to come up. And I want to go, I really do want to."

He'd understand. Aunt Martha was querulous, self-centered, ungenerous, and also well past an age when these characteristics might be expected to improve. Also, her attacks, at least what with florid self-importance she referred to as her attacks, were not in any category that a medical textbook had ever defined. But she was Nan's father's sister, and Nan interpreted the tie as a mandate to take the two-hour trip whenever there was an urgent call.

And this sounded urgent, didn't it? Sweetly discerning, William thought so. He definitely thought so. He said he'd be home by five, and she should call the garage to bring round the car, and this heavenly day, a drive would be the thing for both of them.

Heavenly: right. One of those fall days New York turns out when you can't believe it's sometimes so hot your feet stick sluggishly to the sidewalk or that the chill can ever be cruel enough to penetrate your spine. They'd take turns driving, and after the visit they'd stop at one of those country inns where the owner suggests they've been cooking all day just on the chance that you would stop by—the honeymoon again. Except five minutes later the phone rang and everything within her crumpled.

What he said was he just remembered a meeting of the Pulmonary Studies Society, and he felt obligated to attend.

"But William, Aunt Martha . . ."

"Of course you have to show up."

"I thought you . . . we . . . the two of us . . ."

"Go with Tad," he said. "He just stepped into my office. He says he'd like the drive."

"Tad Collins! William, listen, I can drive alone."

"I don't want you driving alone."

For a second, hearing that gentle forcefulness, a wild idea shook her. He thinks I want to be with Tad. He's heard the rumble of gossip from that dinner and the occasional lunches in the hospital, and the notion has taken hold. He's stepping aside for my pleasure.

No. Absolutely not. William was not a man to step aside. That kind of docile gallantry—I'll take myself out of the picture—it was not his style at all. Assertiveness was built into him, along with decency; skin and bones. If he thought a woman, his woman, was inclined to prefer another man, he'd have it out with her. The head-on confrontation.

Also, he can't possibly think I'm inclined to prefer another man. He has incontrovertible evidence—every night we're together I give him incontrovertible evidence—of how I feel. Don't I? Don't I truly?

"Nan, Tad is just leaving, he'll be there in a minute." Oh, she'd go with Tad, of course; how could she not? But she was angry. Or at least anger was the most readily identifiable of the emotions that swirled within her. He could have come. She had really wanted him to come. This was where he should be, this route that started as expressway, then turned into suburban highway, and narrowed finally into twisting country road. William should be the one sitting next to her, one hand on her knee as he said, should we stop for a bite, you look cute in that hat, shall I put up the window, get a look at that view.

The crossness must have been manifest on her face. "Don't be angry," Tad said. "Hard to change plans in midstream."

Yes, that's it: inflexibility, that symptom of age more telling than the sagging jowls or shortened breath. That's what it means to be old, not a diminution of powers but a reliance on habit. No, we'd better not go; I might miss my ten o'clock bedtime, my four P.M. tea, my cherished electric blanket. Oh, why had he let her think life was going to be expansive and splendid when there must be this stern adherence to the accustomed paths!

Besides, there was something significant about this visit, almost a ceremonial aspect: the first chance either of them had to meet someone from the other's family. They had walked into marriage, each of them, solitary, unattached. William had a sister with whom he said he wasn't close and so it wasn't necessary to invite her because she wouldn't come. And she had Aunt Martha. Aunt Martha, who right this minute might be wheezing her last in that bedroom with the sloping ceiling and the view of apple trees and sky.

Aunt Martha was wheezing, but it was distinctly not a last wheeze, and she'd been moved downstairs. Otherwise it was all the same as the visit Nan had made during the summer. The same irascible look from the woman on the bed, the same faded bed jacket, the same squalid appearance even the trimmest house takes on when it's been occupied for too long by a couple of reclusive women.

"So you got here."

"Hello, Aunt Martha."

"I'm feeling better. I won't die."

"I'm very glad."

"The doctor says I'm doing the right thing. Taking it easy."

Nan proffered a smile. Taking it easy: for years it had been holy writ. Play ball outside; Aunt Martha has to take it easy. Turn down the radio; the doctor told Aunt Martha to take it easy. There was always an amenable doctor, someone willing to intercede between Aunt Martha and the medical mysteries, to prescribe for her what she suggested would be an appropriate prescription.

"The doctor said it was a bad attack."

Nan looked at the querulous face. How could she think of William as old! This is real age, this industrious concern with oneself. Aunt Martha is sixty-eight, and all she deems important in the world is spread before her: medicine, quilt, television, view, the sound of Celia's footsteps in the room outside. A visitor from the city? Well, that's very nice. But would it occur to her that the visitor had worked all day and then driven two hours to get here, that a different segment of world might be elicited from her?

"I got married, Aunt Martha. Remember? I told—"

"Married? That's all right. I hope he can support you."

"Oh, he can, he—"

"Bring him in."

Had she seen them walk up, a man and woman making their tentative way along the dimly lighted path? She'd left Tad in the living room; now she came close to the bed. "Aunt Martha, the man I drove up with, he isn't—" But the obdurate eyelids came down: taking it easy. Okay, what do we do now? Tad appeared in the doorway and cleared his throat, however, and at that sound Aunt Martha's eyes opened, and she said he looks nice, and that finished it.

A real finish because though they stood there, the invalid was asleep. She could stay asleep for hours, her woman said. She was tired. A big day. The doctor said take it—

"We'll go, then. Tell her I said goodbye." She did pause for a second in the overheated living room. Would something be offered: a sandwich, coffee, cheese and crackers, courtesy Aunt Martha? But Aunt Martha's woman had obviously been indoctrinated with Aunt Martha's hospitality, or maybe there really was nothing available—in any case nothing was offered and they were outside.

Out in the sensuous country air that has no relation to what is breathed in the city. Tad opened the car door and said she must be starved. Quarter to eight. She had a right to be starved, but she wasn't; she felt invigorated, lightheaded with relief. How right William had been not to come, not to disrupt his valuable activities just to appease the vanity of a foolish woman. And how bracing not to be angry with him anymore, to have that intrusive weight lifted from her heart. Her good will extended even to Tad, who had seen nothing but her sullen face on the way up and who after all had taken a two-hour drive for no reason except to do a friend a favor. Was she starved? He meant he was; he was entitled to be, and when he said he knew a place near here, not really famous but friends had mentioned it, she didn't have it in her to refuse.

So there they were, at the restaurant she'd envisioned for her and William. One of those places possible only in some remote area where they look at you with wounded eyes if you ask how long will it take. How long? Why, till it's done, you wouldn't want just any ordinary dish, would you? Otherwise why'd you come here and not to that hamburger joint down the road? So sit back, enjoy the view, try some of this wine while you're waiting.

It was nine-thirty when they left, and a quarter to twelve —she checked her watch—when Tad finally parked in front of their apartment, and she didn't object when he said at this late hour he must deliver her directly to William. The way it should be. Lucky her. Cosseted by this personable doctor and then returned, a precious commodity, to her husband.

Her husband whom she couldn't wait to see. Whom in truth she deeply desired. In a way, it was due to Tad. There's a sexual component to time spent with a man. Even though the talk has been determinedly impersonal, the contact held to a studied minimum, the component is there: thighs brush against thighs, hands touch, arms reach out to other arms. And the effect of all that brushing and touching and reaching was to make her languid with longing. After almost six hours with Tad Collins, she couldn't wait to be in bed with William.

She wasn't surprised not to find him in the living room. Almost midnight; he'd have been back from his meeting for an hour, at least, but he'd be awake, he'd be waiting; with that unique telepathy that she was finding out is a function of marriage, the feeling within her would have communicated itself to him, and she said "Just a minute" to Tad and went inside. Then she screamed.

Kept screaming. Even with Tad beside her, his gaze also taking in the blue face of the man on the bed, the contorted mouth, the dangling hands, the empty bottle, she kept screaming.

"Stand back," Tad said. "Stay there."

Illogical. She, a nurse—used to being the first on any scene. She handles it all: the blood that with some willful life of its own has gratuitously spurted, the froth that issues from a throat choking on its own regurgitation. "Just a minute. Step into the waiting room for a minute," she tells the family in her chatelaine voice of kindly efficiency.

But you're not a nurse when your knees tremble, when a disordered heartbeat replaces the usual calm resolve that throbs within you. Stand back? You can't move, you're paralyzed, you hear the peremptory note in that order and your whole strength goes into following it, standing at frantic attention while a doctor, providentially a *real* doctor, takes a pulse, listens to the heart, bends with austere hopefulness over the mouth, turns to you at last.

Dead. He really is dead, her William, in the bed that they have shared for less than two months. Now she does go in; she feels the familiar texture of a hand as she lifts it; she lays her cheek against his rough one. And she sees the note, a torn piece of paper on the blanket next to him.

So I made a mistake—okay, I admit. Being sorry won't help, time won't help, trying to undo things won't help—I see I'll never be free. So I quit.

Chapter

FIVE

IT'S TRUE WHAT THEY SAY ABOUT DEATH. It stupefies you, numbs your powers of reasoning. Especially the death of a beloved, which shifts your mind into torpid acquiescence as it wrenches your feelings more savagely—how well the funeral directors know. There you are, bereft, stupid: Yes. All right. I'll do whatever you say.

Because if her mind hadn't gone soft at the sight of William she'd have done the only sensible thing, which was to destroy that letter. She'd have torn it up and put the pieces down the toilet, and Tad would have been supportive of this reasonable course, and everything would have been different.

Because William didn't mean it. A mistake in marrying her—nothing was going to convince her that he meant it. Oh, it was William, all right—his open handwriting, his lined paper torn out of the notebook on which he jotted ideas. But not his convictions; no, not for a second. Not the conviction of a man who knew in the depths of his contented soul how much his new wife loved him. The delusion rather of one who for some unfathomable reason has momentarily succumbed to the nightmare system of logic that sanctions suicide.

Why, then, should they have read it, the police, the ambulance attendants, the reporters? What right did they have? There were no legal scruples; no doubt, that is, that the death was a suicide. Tad called it, the police doctor verified it, and the autopsy later confirmed it. While she and Tad had sat waiting for the raspberry zabaglione that was the specialty of that unhurried country restaurant, William had lain on their bed and swallowed a bottle of barbiturates.

So no investigative or moral need dictated the display of that letter. Her other letters from William weren't available for inspection, all the notes written in the tender, foolish, whimsical shorthand that a married couple joyfully adopts. They were all around, in the top drawer of her dresser, on a shelf in the kitchen, one of them (Angel, out getting a haircut so you'll love me more and more and more) stuck under an ashtray in the living room—why couldn't this letter remain as hidden, as decently private as those?

Well, it wasn't hidden, and the two policemen who were the first to arrive read it and then held it by the bedside lamp so they could read it again, and when they came finally into the living room where she and Tad were waiting, read it a third time. Something concrete, informative, to direct the course of their questioning.

Because that's what it was, questioning—it struck her as they stood there, she and Tad and these intruders in uniform. They weren't being sorry for her or considering how to take care of her; they were not even treating her with the respect due a grieving wife. They were asking what she had done to make him die. Incredible. They were quizzing her the way they quizzed people who came to the emergency room in the middle of the night with their ugly wounds and unsavory stories. Who? Where? How long? When?

What? An interminable quiz hung up on grotesquely irrelevant details like . . . well, like her aunt's name, would
she spell it, please?

She spelled it. DUNLOP. As in Dunlop. Martha.

"And the address again?" He was younger than she expected, the one putting the questions, with clean-cut features and hair that fell over his eyes as he wrote laboriously
in a lined notebook.

"Look here. I'm a doctor and I've told you what's important." Tad sounded hoarse. Shock had drained the color
from his face—he saw himself, obviously, as her protector,
but she noted his hand tremble as it rested on a chair. "Dr.
Gardiner's been dead about two hours. One hour at the
very least, at which time, as you can surely ascertain, we
were fifty miles away. So is there any reason she has to be
subjected to this inquisition?"

"I think Mrs. Gardiner understands that she's under no
compulsion to say anything." The young policeman spoke
firmly but looked uncertainly over at his partner, who was
older and heavier. Maybe he was being trained and this was
his first crack at sudden death; he was under observation as
much as she was.

"Tad, I want to answer, no reason why not." She went
over to the window. William had loved this view. He used
to stand here, his arm around her, pointing out the varied
wonders. See that building, Angel, with the tall chimney,
an interesting bit of history there. . . . That inimitable zest
for instruction, aimed not at a dozen medical students but
at an attentive wife.

"Okay, I was visiting my aunt, Martha Dunlop, as I said.
Two hours each way, a little longer on the way home. My
husband had wanted to come, but there was this meeting
of some medical society. No, I don't know their address. So
he stayed there I guess two hours, that's how long those

meetings usually take, and then I suppose he came home. Or did he first go out for dinner? God. I don't know." She sat, she suddenly had to sit. Now, was there anything else?

Another murmur from the young policeman. Had her husband ever attempted suicide before?

"No!"

"Did he ever talk about it?"

"Certainly not."

"Well, had he been in low spirits lately?"

She saw Tad's hand clutch more tightly at the chair. "Low spirits? I wouldn't call it that. But he hadn't been himself for a couple of weeks."

"Hadn't been himself in what way?"

She paused. You have to tell them the facts, but surely you're within your rights to withhold that private, indefinable melancholy. "He was tense. He lost his appetite. He didn't sleep well."

"So that explains the pills." A small note of triumph in the policeman's voice: first hurdle cleared.

That explained them, she agreed.

"Had he been taking pills for a long time?"

"He started today."

"I don't understand."

"What's to understand?" her combative voice said. It was intolerable sitting; she stood and then perched, defensive, on the arm of a chair. "Today was my husband's first day of taking sleeping pills."

"Did you know he was going to take them?"

"You mean, did I know he was going to commit suicide?"

"Nan, Nan." Tad did intervene now. "He doesn't mean that."

Well, maybe he didn't; in fact, he looked stunned, the young policeman, letting the notebook hang limp from his hand. She drew her breath and said since her husband hadn't been sleeping well, they had agreed that some medication might help.

"So they weren't even in the house until today, those pills."

"No, they weren't."

"Did you know he was going to bring them home?"

"No."

"You weren't aware that—"

She hesitated; they'll find out anyhow. "What I meant was, he didn't bring them. That is, I did."

"You brought them?" Another of those speculative looks between the two policemen, another reminder from Tad that she's under no obligation to answer anything.

"Tad, I know; it's okay, really. Well, the pills. My husband wanted them"—Did he? Did he really? Oh, God, something else to think about—"so he wrote the prescription and gave it to me and I had it filled at the hospital commissary, the one down on the third floor—I'm sure you'll check up; we all buy our drugs there."

"All? Are you also on the staff?"

"I'm a nurse."

"I see."

What does he see, this apprentice policeman on his maiden investigation? What's he writing, the pencil crawling like a diligent insect across the page? That she doesn't belong here? That these aren't customary digs for a nurse, this apartment with the two curved couches and the built-in stereo and the view that was William's special joy?

"Look, what's the difference about the pills? I mean, they'll do an autopsy, don't they always? You'll know exactly how much and what he took; isn't that the routine in suicide . . ." She knew she was shouting. An autopsy on William: in that white-tiled room, the definitive slit down the front, the organs lifted out one by one. Shouting and also crying, because now the older policeman spoke up. He had a nice voice with a faint foreign accent, and he said they didn't want to get her more upset. They realized it was a terrible time for her. They'd try to get it over very fast. The doctor would come and then—

The doctor was here now; she heard the elevator, then the bustle at the door, then the apologetic coughs because there's no tactful way to carry a stretcher through a living room. For an interval then, peace; she and Tad could stand silent while the others went into the bedroom. Paying attention to William at last. Maybe arranging those importunate hands. Wiping the stained mouth. Straightening the hair over that noble forehead—services she could comprehend. And meanwhile talking, consulting; she could hear the grave collective mumble.

It did not, though, get over fast enough. The young policeman came out and said Dr. Alexis had confirmed the timing. Dead well over an hour. However—a diffident shake of his head—the estimate on Dr. Gardiner's arrival home had been somewhat different from hers. Did she say her husband went for a couple of hours to a meeting? Because Dr. Alexis talked to the elevator man on the way up, and this attendant said Dr. Gardiner had been home by six; the man remembered because he himself was just then going off for supper.

"Six o'clock?"

"What he said."

She sat again. William, why'd you do this to me, bring me here and then abandon me in a strange country where I don't speak the language or know the customs, I'm not even sure which signposts are important and which aren't.

And why are they looking at her? A discrepancy in the time a suicidal man came home: are they really going to make something of it? Mrs. Gardiner is not at present a suspect; however, she did go out with another man when she knew her husband was in low spirits, and she did persuade him to take sleeping pills—no, they don't know that, strike it—she did purchase the bottle of pills with which he killed himself, and she did furthermore state that her husband was going to a meeting when on investigation it turns out...

An investigation that made sense only in terms of that letter. "So I made a mistake." Ah, but she had made the bigger mistake. She had left it, that message from William to her, to become clue number one, so when the policemen and medical men at last walked out, that sheet of torn paper was slipped into a folder and carried off with as much finicky deliberation as was used to maneuver the stretcher past the curved couches, and along the wall where William had said they must build more bookshelves, and up against the cabinet that concealed the marvels of his hi-fi equipment, and out finally into the hall.

Well, who really understands these things? Maybe that terrible deed enacted by William aroused some masochistic feelings of which she was only dimly aware; she knew she wasn't guilty, but in some obscure part of her psyche she knew she must be guilty, and so she let the letter slip into the public domain to make sure she would receive the punishment that was her due. True? Not true? She didn't know: to practice as a first-rate nurse, it is not necessary to have boned up on Freud.

In any case, the letter did enter the public domain, and God knows she was punished. How does information insidiously spread, like acid rain, like radioactive dust? A midwest chimney spouting black smoke poisons fish in a lake half a continent away, and by the same implacable mechanism, the words on a torn piece of paper are disseminated so everyone in the hospital knows what was written on them.

Yes. Everyone. She was back at the hospital a week after William's death, and a day later the nursing supervisor called her down. What she said, that good busy woman who obviously was not acting on her own, who must have checked with the authorities before she spoke, was that it was a very unfortunate business. She said perhaps Miss Dunlop would be happier in some other line of work. She said she realized of course no definite charges had been pressed. She said finally, after Nan had opened her mouth and closed it, they would understand if Miss Dunlop wanted to finish out the month.

Her walking papers? Not exactly. Besides, if it came to that, she could fight it; naturally she could. Look at all the nurses who would defend her, rally round her; who in their hearts held tight the truth about her. She saw Rosanne go into the linen room that afternoon and hurried after her, but another voice stopped her at the door. ". . . don't mind that she saw her way to get filthy rich, I really don't. It's just that she's ruined it for all of us. Loused it up but good. I mean, if a nurse so much as smiles at a doctor now, well, you know what they'll immediately think. Honestly, why'd she have to do it, treat him that way? She could have waited a year, a really nice man like Dr. Gardiner, she didn't have to—"

That incisive voice, was it Paula? That nurse who was so gentle, so unfailingly patient and resourceful with the woman in 923 who was dying of cervical cancer? And why didn't Rosanne answer? Rosanne, her dear friend, who heard her moans of obsessive passion and helped with the strategic maneuvering and stood next to her while sick with love she listened to Dr. Gardiner lecture.

Next day Rosanne came over to her table in the cafeteria. Glory be. Now they could talk, work their way back to the footing of trust and intimacy. Rosanne stood holding a tray. "Oh, wow, I see you got that salad. Two thirty-five for just a few pieces of apple and some nuts; it really is an outrage. I just bought an orange for forty cents, absolutely as much to eat, and you save a dollar and . . ."

She looked up at those pretty, sharp features. "Rosanne, listen. We haven't really had time to—that is, how about meeting me after work? We can go for tea."

"Tea. That sounds okay. No, wait. Someone told me about this sale of winter coats at a place downtown, those sheepskin ones that usually cost the earth, only here they're sixty percent off retail. And my old one's impossible. So if I can grab one before they're all gone—"

All right, now she knows. She's an alien. Money: it surrounds you, encases you, like a space suit cuts you off from normal communication. How could she have pursued an honorable course when its final result was to leave her, a nurse, thus amply buttressed by money?

And it's a lot of money, more than she had any idea when with innocent bliss she aligned herself to William's life. She had her first glimmer of how much when she spoke to William's investment counselor, one of those men courteous of your ignorance, respectful of your position, cognizant of his own good fortune in having you for client. With pompous deference he led her through the unfamiliar paths: tax exempts, diversity, double A ratings, cash flow, money funds. William had been conservative in his ventures, he supposed that she also? Well, yes, he understands. No changes. Naturally, no changes. A great responsibility, this kind of portfolio—this said with a sly look, his only allusion to the unmentionable fact that she was distinctly poor before making the match that left her inordinately rich. In any case, premature to talk about changes until she has met with her lawyer—Victor Hemmings, right? He'll give her an idea of the whole picture; has she seen him yet?

"We have an appointment at five-thirty on Thursday."

"Good man, Hemmings. You're lucky to have him."

"Listen. Do I have to see him? I mean, couldn't we . . . that is, by phone . . ."

"Mrs. Gardiner, the executor of your husband's estate! All the new decisions—you'll be going steady with him, so to speak."

"I will?"

"Oh my, yes. The most important person in your life from this time on."

"I see." Well, maybe it wouldn't be so terrible. Everything in her life had turned upside down. The people she had reason to think were her dearest friends had made clear that they believed the worst about her; maybe her erstwhile enemy would have the bigness of spirit to turn himself into an ally. It was possible, wasn't it? Barely possible?

No, it was not possible, she knew as soon as she came in. There was nothing overt, just the set of his face and the blandness of his voice as he began talking about her estate. A sizable estate; William had had a lucrative practice, and his investment counselors had obviously had a skilled and lucky hand. All very conservatively invested, as perhaps she knew: bonds with triple A ratings, some small real-estate tax shelters, money funds . . . the arcane vocabulary which was fast becoming less arcane.

". . . big responsibility, but no immediate decisions are necessary. In any case, you're in no position to decide anything until the will is probated, which can take two or even three months depending on the press of business and perhaps some other factors at Surrogate's Court. A small number of bonds is due next month, but the money can be invested in short-term treasury bills which now pay in the neighborhood of . . ."

She's getting the hang of it: these whirpools of talk in which estimates about money lead to warnings about responsibility, which lead to tributes to the brains or luck of those who have made the money grow, which lead back again to estimates about those hefty sums. Circular. Endless.

Except this one did end; it ended with a sudden shift to something else, and the juxtaposition between the subject of her newly acquired affluence and the next subject so shook her that for a second she could hardly breathe. What Victor said was he'd been looking into the circumstances of the way she and William had met.

She sat silent. William was all around them, his imposing body and exuberant face now at the window, now in this comfortable chair where he'd sat beside her, now close to the door past which the typewriter of that conscientious secretary sat silent and shrouded. Nan, if anything happens to me, you'll be in good hands.

"That is, I've been talking to some of the people at the hospital about the way you got to know him."

"People at the hospital, I see."

"From what I gather, you laid a very deliberate siege. The whole thing was cleverly planned. Every time William turned a corner or sat down to read a chart or went into a room, there you were—he couldn't help but see you."

That long, narrow, thoughtful face—it was the way the brainy boys in college had looked, the ones who wrote learned articles in the lit magazine or stood up to ask obscure questions in Soc. 5-6. She barely knew them; it had been the basketball star, the first guitarist in a rock group who went for that cute Nan Dunlop. Was this what they turned into, those brains—hard, mean-spirited, mistrustful?

"This is crazy. You didn't have to go snooping around. Why didn't you ask me, I'd have saved you all that trouble. Yes. True. I did go after him. I saw him and I—" Fell in love; don't say it; her mouth would choke on the words. "I paid someone, another nurse, to let me work her end of the floor where he had his patients. I went without lunch because that was when he came to do rounds. To get the head nurse on my side, I took care all alone of just about the hardest case, someone with fistulas and his wound wouldn't heal, but that wasn't why the other nurses hated to go in, it was because even sick as he was he—Oh, what do you care? Yes. The answer is yes, I pulled every trick so I could be near him. That enough? Anything else you'd like to know?"

"Yes." The intent face leaned forward, next to the picture of his son, that sensitive dark-eyed child who resembled him. "Why couldn't you give him a year? A man of sixty-seven. One contented, fulfilled year, before you started playing around with younger men."

Funny. Just what Paula had said. One year—did they really suppose that skimpy time was all that William deserved! "If you're talking about that night, the dinner for Dr. Davis, William made me go—he had gout; he said—"

"William never had gout in his life."

She was silent. Maybe he didn't. The sudden suspicion struck her that maybe he didn't. William, why did you lie to me?

"I told you not to injure his spirit. If I'd known you were going to assault his self-respect—"

"You have no right to say that."

"As I explained, Miss Dunlop, I loved him. The kind of friendship William and I had confers more rights than I'm afraid you can understand."

My name isn't Miss Dunlop, it's Mrs. Gardiner. She said nothing.

"Oh, William was no saint, he led a full and varied life —he'd have been the first to say it. But marriage was a big commitment for him, one in which his pride was inextricably bound up. He took for granted it would also be a commitment for his wife. As you must have figured out when you made your plans, he wasn't prepared to have her spending her evenings with other men."

She went over to the window: miles and miles of offices like this one. Maybe this was the way lawyers talked in all of them, the steely voices uttering the unscrupulous accusations. "The night William died—you know, everyone knows—he told me he had a meeting; that's why he couldn't come with me to my aunt's."

"That nonexistent meeting. Like the fugitive gout."

"Are you trying to imply that William didn't tell me he was going to a meeting?" She stopped; of course it was what he was trying to imply, and how could she prove otherwise, how?

"I also wonder about those sleeping pills," Victor said. "I happen to know William never took them; he had strong feelings against taking them."

"Listen, William wrote the prescription—"

"I don't doubt it," Victor said flatly. "So there he was, with those unaccustomed sleeping pills, sitting home with them from six o'clock on, while his wife didn't get home until—"

"I know what time I got home."

"Four hours after you left your aunt's. With whom you confined your visit to something under fifteen minutes."

Why was she listening? He had no kind of authority over her; she didn't have to sit here mesmerized. "Okay, so we stopped for dinner on the way home."

"That was some stop," Victor said. "At a time when your husband was waiting. Or maybe you didn't think of him as your husband, and that's why you passed off Dr. Collins as your husband to your aunt."

"Oh, Christ, do you really want to know how that happened?" But he didn't; of course he didn't. She drew herself up. "Listen, I went through all this with the police, if they were satisfied . . ."

But she didn't exactly go through all this because Victor knew things the police didn't. He knew about William's aversion to sleeping pills, for instance. He knew that William's excuse about gout was a false one. And now it turned out he knew about Aunt Martha's mistake in taking Tad to be her husband. Victor must have gone up there himself to uncover this squalid little fact. What did he expect to accomplish by playing detective on his own? What was he planning to do with all this information?

"Is that your idea?" he said. "The police were satisfied?"

Well, of course she knows the police aren't satisfied, but neither do they have the grounds for an accusation, just as the hospital doesn't have the right to fire her outright. But she needn't answer because now he switches subjects again.

". . . not sure if you're familiar with the duties of an executor. No? To put it in the simplest terms, the executor has the responsibility for collecting the assets of the estate and holding them or investing them on a temporary basis until the creditors make their claims and taxes and fees are paid, after which everything is turned over to the beneficiaries. But of course it's not that simple; even in a case like this where no claims of any substance are expected and only one beneficiary is involved, it's not entirely simple. Decisions have to be made; the nature of investments changes; consultations are in order. Consultations, that is to say, between the beneficiary, who is you, and the executor, who is me."

Going steady. I know. Conscious of his gaze, she remained at the window. She was wearing a tan suit, with the blouse William had bought on their honeymoon. "What I always wanted to do," he had said. "Go to the snazziest store in a foreign city and buy something and have my wife put it right on." She buttoned the jacket up to the collar: Was Victor really going to keep on with this colorless presentation, as if nothing had happened between them?

No, he was not going to keep on with this colorless presentation. ". . . in short, an ongoing relationship. However, with my having the kind of doubts about you that I do have, that kind of relationship would be intolerable. Intolerable to me and also, I daresay, to you." A pause, but only to take a breath. "I don't say all this lightly, you understand. William imposed on me a position of great trust. It goes strongly against me to disregard his wishes. But the circumstances being what they are, I have no alternative except to petition the court to relieve me of my position."

Another rejection. She wouldn't want anything to do with him, God knows she wouldn't, but still, here it is, she's being rejected once more.

". . . won't of course be without adequate representation. In instances like this, the court appoints either a substitute executor or a public administrator, but in any case it won't make a difference to your financial stability—Just a minute, not quite finished."

Not finished! Christ, would he go on forever, all of it coming out in a homogenized stream, the insinuations that she plotted to kill William, and the solicitude about her finances, and the correct legalities, and the clear-cut explanations, all so smoothly presented that if someone who didn't know the language were to hear that expressionless voice and see his calm, thoughtful face, they would conclude that this was any talk between lawyer and client, a routine discussion in this dignified room.

". . . should also mention that since the same reservations

that mitigate against my being your executor hold true for our firm representing you in future, I assume you'll want to find new counsel. I've made up a list of appropriate firms, and my secretary will send it to you in a day or so —of course you're free to use the suggestions or not, as you wish. I may add that since an estate like yours adds up to a very remunerative case, I hardly think you'll have trouble finding suitable counsel who—"

"Oh, stop. Just stop all this idiocy. I swear, the way you sit there, with that fancy talk and the detective work, so pious, but you have everything wrong. Everything. You don't even know why I married him or what our marriage was like; you haven't the faintest idea. Well, good. I don't want you to know. I wouldn't want any feelings of mine exposed to your nasty mind. And I'm glad you're doing that whatever you call it. Petition. Because if you think I'd ever come to you for advice or help, if you really think that. William didn't make many mistakes, but, oh God, he made one about you, he certainly did."

She walked quickly down the hall, past offices with the same deep rugs, dark paneling, well-chosen prints as Victor's. All empty. No secretaries in the alcoves, no gray-haired partners behind the desks, and it occurred to her that this was why he'd set their appointment at five-thirty. So if she made a scene, if she did anything so unbecoming, there would be no witnesses to it. Well, fakeout on Victor Hemmings. She was going to make a scene, all right, it was just coming to her what kind of scene she was going to make, but it would be at her own good time and under her own well-chosen auspices.

Chapter
SIX

"NOT AT PRESENT A SUSPECT," she said.

"What's that?"

"What I am. Not at present a suspect but."

She was talking to Tad, her only friend. She'd been the one to call him; by tacit consent, they'd avoided one another after William's death, but the day after she saw Victor she called him; she had to see him, she said. Well, sure, Nan darling, he wanted to see her too—then his voice tapered off. Exactly: thinking the same thing she was: Where should they meet? Not in the hospital, surely, where everyone was watching, misconstruing; never again could she and Tad sit at that corner table in the cafeteria while the clattering noise went on inconsequentially around them. And not in William's apartment, what she always would think of as William's apartment, because the half dozen doctors who knew her and might see Tad in the elevator would put on his presence an even worse misconstruction. And not in some out-of-the-way place because wouldn't they then appear even more guilty: Look how they're still sneaking around to be together, the two of them.

"Maybe it's not such a good idea after all," she said wanly.

"Look, Nan. You want to see me? Well, I definitely want to see you. You get out at three, right? Well, take a bus over to Central Park, you know that statue on the avenue with the benches around . . . ?"

But even the most hospitable park bench can be discouraging on a blowy day, so here they were, after all, at the back table of an obscure bar on an unlikely side street, while Tad told her to stop looking around; no one was going to see them and suppose they did?

"They'll think the worst," she said. "Except there's no worst left for them to think."

"Nan, take it easy."

She ran her finger around the chilled top of her glass. "The nursing supervisor called me down. Amy Harkness, a very decent woman. She said maybe I ought to think about some other field than nursing. She said it in the tone that implied I—"

"I can imagine her tone," Tad said.

"She said I was perfectly welcome to finish out the month."

He banged down his glass. "They haven't a leg to stand on. You can fight them—"

"And one of the men from public relations stopped me in the hall this morning. He wondered was there anything I could tell him that would enable them to cast me in a more favorable light."

"What'd you—Nan, stop looking around; no one we know is coming in."

"I said there was nothing that would enable them to cast me in a more favorable light."

He was quiet while the waiter squeezed past them to get to the next table. "You don't have to take that kind of treatment. This is your hospital. You've been there—how many years? Three? Four? Enough so everyone knows you, thinks highly of you. . . ."

"They thought more highly of Dr. Gardiner, and they've

read the newspapers, and they know I married him to get his money."

"Hold it—"

"I don't even want to work there. You don't believe it, but it's the truth. Why should I work at a place where no one will talk to me, no one? The other day I walked into the nurses' lounge for a cigarette and the three nurses who were there stood up and walked out. And in the cafeteria . . ." Another pause; the waiter was coming back. "You know what's worst of all? I can't talk about William. About how wonderful he was. I mean, that's the privilege you have when someone dies, isn't it? You can talk and talk; it makes you feel, okay, not better, but stronger. Well, if I even mention William to someone, they clear their throat and look sideways before they slink away. You know the old movies? There's always this mistress dressed all in black at the man's funeral, and the rightful family looks at her and whispers. Who's that one? What's she doing here? Well, that one is me. Illicit. That's how I feel. Any grief I have about William is illicit; no one would believe in it. I can't even cry. I mean, what if they thought my tears were a fake? Tad, I'm sorry. I didn't mean to blow my top."

Tad sat very still; light from the inadequate ceiling fixture shone on the pained eyes and angry mouth. "Listen. I'm going to call a press conference. Make it absolutely clear that William engineered that final night himself. First told us he was going to a meeting, and then asked me if I would take you to your aunt's."

But he stopped. They had been through this before; for Dr. Collins to say more in her defense than he'd already said could only be harmful. Add a corroborative stamp to the ungenerous speculations.

"God. You feel so helpless. If there were something we could do."

She picked a pretzel out of the plastic dish. Actually there was something she could do—the idea beat at her with chilling insistence. She could give up the money. Turn it over to that society that had been slated to get it before she came into the picture. "Young Widow Asserts She Wants No Part of Dr. Gardiner's Estate."

But she did want it; she wanted it with an intensity that surprised her. Money—she hadn't thought of it one way or other when she and William got married. It was simply another convenience: the reason they could stay at the best hotels or order with lordly casualness at the most extravagant restaurants. Part of William: an asset like his exuberant laugh and expansive good looks and easy skill on the dance floor.

But now the laugh and the looks were gone, and she had only the money. Her possession, her treasure, her security blanket. Her *right:* despite Victor's objections, an asset that could be deeded over. It had made all the trouble, oh, she knew that: Had William never written that will, she wouldn't now be blamed for his death. And maybe money wasn't even good for one's character, it brought out whatever acquisitive streaks were latent, or it blunted ambition, or something. Well, okay. Men who used to keep slaves knew how deleterious slavery was; they wrote against it, spoke against it, enlisted in causes that tried to undermine it, but still they hung on to their own slaves, and in the same way, having weighed everything, she intended to hang on to her money. Hers.

Besides, if she gave it up now, wouldn't that look as if she were simply trying to prove her innocence? Like a defense from Tad Collins, it would corroborate the most insidious accusations.

And besides all that, right now she needed it. Had to have it for the new direction her life was going to take. She looked across the small table. "Tad, listen. I didn't ask you to meet me because I needed sympathy. I mean, I do need it, God knows, but the thing is, I wanted to ask your advice; you're the only one I can ask. That is, about my plans."

He put down his drink. There was some gray in his sandy hair, for the first time she noticed it, but it didn't make him look older; it seemed an anomaly, rather, above the round pleasant features. He looked baffled. Her plans?

"Did you think I was going to sit back and take it? Nan, the suspect? Tarred for life? There's too much that's inexplicable—no thanks, no more to drink. Inexplicable," she said again. "First sending the two of us off to that dinner by saying he had gout when he didn't." She paused but didn't mention Victor, who had been the reason why she checked. "Not an instance, Dr. Leroy is positive. Well, why then? And that other night that no one will credit, but you and I know is for real, why again? Why wouldn't he come with me to my aunt's? Why'd he invent that meeting? What was eating him?"

"Some upset at the office maybe," Tad said inconclusively.

"He wasn't that kind. Not William. Oh, there were cases that bothered him; once in a while he'd mention them. A woman with I think tumor of the pleura—should they treat it with radiation or chemotherapy? But he didn't bring the office home, not ever. He just knew he was the best there was, but when he was off duty he was off duty, that was what was so great about him—no, I'm not crying."

Not crying, but her voice wound down. An interval of silence here was different from one in the cafeteria. There when you stopped talking you were caught up in the surrounding bustle: the droning talk of people at the next table, the chair pushed back by a doctor whose beeper had just sounded, the probing look from someone holding a full tray while searching for an empty seat. Here your own quiet defined you, enclosed you; there was a couple at a nearby table, a woman in a shawl, a man who hadn't bothered to remove his raincoat, but there was no link; their mumble didn't carry across the intervening feet.

"And then why did he commit suicide? Why? That letter is no answer; it's worse than no answer," she said in a voice that sounded strident in her own ears. "A mistake. *So I made a mistake.* I've been going over and over those terrible words. We took for granted the mistake was marrying me. I did. You did—"

"I didn't say—"

"No, but you believed it. Tad, I don't blame you, you were half crazy, William lying there, your old friend, maybe you could still save him, and then the police—Tad, I'm all *right.*" She sat with hands folded primly on the small table: Look how full of reasonable sanity I am. "*So I made a mistake, okay I admit.* Know what I think? The mistake was not related to our marriage; it had nothing to do with me at all. It was something else."

"Like what?"

The couple at the next table stood up; she waited while the ends of raincoat and shawl swept past her. "Like something that happened long ago, and for some reason the happiness with me—because we were happy, we really were—well, that happiness troubled him and he felt culpable—Oh, Tad, don't look at me like that. It's wild, of course. But there was something. Yes, he was upset, but it wasn't about his practice, and it wasn't, I could swear, about me; it was just something needling him, dragging at his spirits so once we came home from our trip he was different; he never quite got near that pure joy of the weeks before."

That encompassing silence again. The table legs were uneven; when she leaned her elbow on one side, she could hear the ice clinking against the glasses. "That mistake," Tad said at last. "Do you think it was something in medicine? A diagnosis, say, that later turned out to have been ill advised? Take that case you mentioned. Mesothelioma. Tumor of the pleura, as you called it. Because it's riddled with ambiguity. You can toss a coin. Heads we treat it with radiation. Tails it's chemotherapy. And God knows we all—"

"No, I don't think that. He was too reasonable, William was. Too imbued with the sense of his own enormous worth. He'd never brood for years over an honest blunder. No, I think—Tad, this is hard to say, I know how you respected him."

"Go on."

"I think something to do with a woman. A girl. You must know, William didn't keep it secret, there were lots of women before me. And there must have been even more, I mean, it's a natural inference, when he was younger. All those years in Washington. Well"—another jolt from that unsteady table—"suppose a girl had an abortion, a girl he'd been going with, and she died."

"Girls don't die from abortions."

"Thirty years ago they did. Maybe even twenty. There was all that business. Sleazy practitioners, blindfolds, money passed under the table—okay, I know what you're going to say. Doctors have the resources of a hospital. Well, even there, things can go wrong; haven't we both seen it? So let's say the girl died, or was maimed—the girl who expected him to marry her—oh, who needs the scenario? Just the old old story."

He gave a long, speculative sigh. Did it mean he agreed? He didn't agree?

"Or let's say she was maimed in another way. Yes, now I think of it; it's even more likely she was maimed in some

other way. Her spirit, that is. Look. There's a woman doctor right now in anesthesiology, everyone knows who she
is. Well, she and William had a thing for a while, and her
husband got wind of it and divorced her, but by that time
William had drifted away so now she has no one—it would
have to be more than that, of course. I'm talking about
someone brutally hurt. Her life ruined."

Another pause while a new couple, two men this time,
settled themselves at the nearby table. Then he said it was
a little hard to think of William doing something hurtful.
Leaving a girl in the lurch. That William. So compassion-
ate.

"But that's the point. In my scenario, he wouldn't have
found out till the damage was done. Whatever the damage
was. Besides, there's something else." She twirled her glass;
it was easier not to look up. "Tad, a couple of times when
he was at his lowest, melancholy almost, just at those bleak
moments he said I reminded him of someone. A girl he
knew long ago. So you see."

He did see: in a sense, the burden more sharply focused
—his face exuded discernment. But all he asked was how
did she think she was going to locate this hypothetical girl
from ten or twenty or maybe even thirty years back?

"I'm going to read all his papers. Medical records, letters,
a diary he kept for years—till now I couldn't bring myself
to touch them, but I will. And I'm going down there. Don't
look so surprised; as soon as I tell the police, I really am."

"What's the police got to do with it?"

"Oh, didn't I mention that? They want me to keep them
informed, their cute language, about any plans to leave
town."

"But . . . I mean . . ."

"I brought home those sleeping pills, after all. The ones
I coaxed him to take so I could inherit his money—Tad,

forget it. It's just one more thing. They didn't say I couldn't go. So day after tomorrow, I leave. That hospital—your hospital too, isn't it?—where he worked for so long, I'll start asking questions there."

Tad looked sick, but all he said was people weren't always keen on answering the kind of question she had in mind.

When she moved her elbow, the glass tottered on the edge of the table. "I've always been able to get people to talk; it's one of the reasons I'm a good nurse. Does that sound conceited? It's a fact. Patients unwind when I'm taking care of them; they tell me things other nurses never get near finding out. Oh, I don't mean I sit having cozy chitchat; no nurse would last five minutes if she did. But there's such a thing as giving proper care, attending to the bedsores, say, and also making clear that you're an interested listener. And they can bear their miseries better that way. Even if what they have is hopeless, it does them good. I mean it invigorates them; it really does, to know someone wants to listen."

She was the one being invigorated. How tight she had been, walking around with her hurt gaze and set mouth in the company of all those people to whom it had not been possible to talk because they would not believe her—how she had needed this session with Tad!

"And if they won't talk, if they absolutely resist, I'll tell them"—she thought a second—"I'll say I'm writing a book about him. William Gardiner, Caring Internist. Anyhow, I have to do it, I can't stay in this trap forever. So will you help me, will you?"

His large warm friendly hand came down over hers. Did she really have to ask? What else was Tad Collins here for except to help her in this tortured time?

Chapter
SEVEN

WELL, HELP. Even from someone as caring and knowl-
edgeable as Tad. Oh, with the most perfect kindness he can
get you over the logistical hurdles—motels, neighborhoods,
transportation, time—all that solicitous attention that
makes you forget the world is against you. But in the end
you're still on your own.

She was on her own two days later, driving down to
Washington. Or, rather, on this first day driving halfway
down, because for her first stop she was going to see William's sister, who lived in a small city in northeast Pennsylvania. A predictable small city, the kind whose good days
have long been over—getting off the expressway, she drove
through streets with small frame houses, abandoned stores,
untidy yards, hotels that advertised ROOMS in flickering
signs down their unpainted fronts.

She drove slowly. William's birthplace. A gangling teen-
ager, he carried his books and lunch box into that high
school at the corner. In winter he disregarded the No Skat-
ing sign on the lake. He held hands with his first date at that
boarded-up movie house. Possible, wasn't it? She couldn't
be sure; he had never told her anything about the place. So
far as she knew, he'd grown up here and left, and that was
that.

But his sister had stayed on, the sister whom he hadn't

bothered to invite to the wedding reception. She'll probably give me a hard time, Nan had thought when she
phoned yesterday. She'll have all kinds of excuses why
she can't see me, and I won't blame her. But surprise! the
sister had been wholly welcoming. "Come on along,
honey, be good to meet you. You'll be driving? Take the
right fork where Main and Cleveland meet, then a mile or
so on Cleveland, then sharp left up the hill to Adams,
then a quarter of a mile to the place with the high black
gate and stone columns."

The place with black gate and stone columns was a second surprise. She drove through an acre of landscaped
curves, parked on a circular driveway, went up three banks
of steps, and looked at an imposing red brick house. Maybe
a mistake. Could William's sister really live here, this place
where everything spelled show, spelled money?

But it was William's sister who opened the door. Oh,
God, was it ever William's sister. The large face, the craggy
features, the gaze going over her with blue-eyed clarity—
William! However, a woman's voice saying, "Come on in,
you must be cold; like I said on the phone, of course a
pleasure—I know. You think I look like William."

Didn't just look like—standing serene and proprietary in
the doorway, the woman had brought William back. Nan
gave a stupefied nod.

"They always said so. All the time we were growing up.
Two peas in a pod. Only thing is, the pod was one that
happened to be becoming to him. He was a charmer from
the word go. Me, I was a young girl with a boyish face, and
then I was a middle-aged woman with a man's distinguished face, and now I'm old, worse luck, I still have a face
that would look good on a man."

What could you say? All true. The expansive solidity that
had imbued William with princely charm made his sister

look somber and unfeminine. But her voice moved at its own agreeable clip. "Anyhow, nothing wrong with your looks. Imagine William at his age getting a pretty thing like you—I have to hand it to him. Honey, give me your coat. Now. What can I get you? Coffee? A drink?"

She followed William's sister and said coffee would be fine; she'd be driving again after she left.

The woman went to the door and consulted with someone—then a maid came in with rolls, jam, coffee, cake for one, soda and ice for the other—a production to keep them both occupied for a few minutes. William's sister poured herself a drink, and then she looked up with the gaze that was William's, that made your heart stop with its closeness to William. "Honey, I'm glad you're here. A little talk so we get to know each other, I couldn't wish for anything better. But the way you sounded on the phone—you didn't come for a little talk, did you?"

Nan put down her cup. "Look, Mrs. Mitchell—"

"Jeanette. We're by way of being sisters-in-law."

Dear lord. Sister-in-law to this woman with the lined face and gray hair and sagging bust—it puts her marriage in a whole new perspective. But she sat straight and said Jeanette knew how William had died, didn't she?

"They told me. Jesus. I know, but I can't really believe it. William committing suicide. He was always so sure of himself. Top of the world." She finished her drink and poured another. "Or maybe he changed. I haven't set eyes on him for ten years. Not since he came home for our father's funeral."

"He didn't change. He was still top of the world."

"Then it's worse. To give you a rotten deal like that, do something so cruel. I'd never think my own brother—"

"But that's it. He wasn't cruel. He was the kindest, the most tender—no, I'm all right, really." She felt Jeanette's

arm around her. Sympathy from a concerned woman—she
could use a little of that.

She could use it, and it would just mess everything up.
She said that was why she was here, just because William's
suicide had been so out of character. So she was going to
talk to everyone who knew him. Jeanette was the first.

"I don't get it."

"Listen. We were married for two months, and I knew
him for maybe three months before that. And I'm not so
dumb. I'm a nurse—I understand about people. And I
never heard anything in those five months to make me
remotely think he was a candidate for killing himself. But
he did that, William really did, and he also acted in some
very peculiar ways the last couple of weeks, and I want to
know why. What don't I know about? What went on in his
life before I met him?"

William's sister gave her a heavy stare. "You mean, you
really think you can do a detective number on William's
past? A young girl like you?"

"I will do it. I'm on my way to Washington now because
that's where he worked for most of his life—I have my car
outside. Actually, William's car, of course. I have clothes in
it for an indefinite stay. Also, I have a motel room reserved
on an open-ended basis. Afterwards I'll go back to New
York and start pumping the people there."

Jeanette looked out the window—was she sizing up the
car, trying to draw from it some inference about the kind
of person her brother had turned into? "Honey, how old
are you? Twenty-six? Jesus. I'm almost forty years older
than you. I was two years younger than William. Well,
never mind all that." She came back and, despite her bulk,
seated herself gracefully. William's grace. "Tell me something. Did William leave you his money? All of it? Oh,
don't go getting all uptight; I like you, I'm on your side,"

she said in her brisk voice. "I understand that doctors, big New York doctors, specialists, they make a mint—am I right? Well, take it. Enjoy it. Have yourself a ball—it couldn't go for better use. Then after a while, six months say—okay, wait a year, if you insist, and then marry someone else. He'll be out there, that new fellow. Even without all that dough, he'd be out there. So give him a break. Give yourself a break. The thing to remember, with money you're in the driver's seat," Jeanette said, all amiable forcefulness, and for a second she even sounded like William. "You don't have to go spending your looks and youth tracking down some old man's secrets."

Well, it had validity, that argument. Could it instill in her such a sense of felicitous contentment if it didn't have validity? In the driver's seat—for sure. She didn't have to fight to stay on in a hospital where she was looked upon with malign distrust. If it came to that, she didn't have to stay in nursing altogether; surely there were other fields on which she could expend her talents. Long ago, before she'd set her life on its present course, she'd gone through a period of considering them. Art history. Clinical psychology. Something else—she forgot. Years of training needed, but if you had inherited a mint—who didn't know it?— anything was possible.

She arranged the spoon and fork on her cake plate. "I can't," she said. "I have to do this. I have to because"—the fork was out of alignment—"they think I married him for his money."

"Who's they?"

"Everyone. The police. The man who was William's lawyer. People at the hospital. My friends—I mean, they used to be my friends. I conned him into rewriting his will, and then I made him miserable so he killed himself, and I walked off with the loot. If they could put me in jail, they would, but they have no grounds for putting me in jail—it seems it's not a crime to drive your husband to suicide. Don't laugh. When you look at it one way, they're not being so unreasonable. I mean, I really was out with another man the night that he—anyhow, that's what it looks like, that I very cleverly staged the whole thing, but appearances can lie," she finished in a burst of breathless defiance.

"You're telling me," William's sister said.

"I was only with that man because William—"

"Honey, you don't have to explain to me, I believe you. You married him because you loved him; why wouldn't I believe that? Everyone always loved him. Our parents, the teachers, the girls in school, me. Me, you said it; I adored him. So of course you'd fall for him, stands to reason. I bet you had fun with him too." She asked it kindly, not salaciously, but her meaning was clear.

Nan nodded. Yes. Lots of fun.

"Think of it. That William. Sixty-seven years old and still able to give a girl a good time in bed. Well, honey, I see you're as stubborn as that piece of marble over there; you're going to persist in your hopeless project. But what I don't see, where do I come in? What can I tell you that William didn't?"

"Actually, he never talked about the past." It was true; another way in which public opinion had been wrong. Rosanne had cautioned her, all the nurses had: didn't she know what older people were like? They fed on the past, their favorite topic, just about, an interminable reminiscence about the way things used to be. And the idea did give her pause. She remembered her father, giving scrupulous attention to bygone dates, numbers, street addresses, as if with gratuitous veracity to restore some ancient era: "That was when we were living at 784 McLoude Street, and your Aunt Martha was around the corner at 19 Oak;

only in August we had to move to that two-family house at 3 Dover Place; no, it was July, July tenth, I remember distinctly because . . ." Exactly the opposite turned out to be the case with William, however; he winced if someone tried to head him down those nostalgic paths and turned the conversation around with a resoluteness that had seemed to her at once estimable and dashing. Now she said anything Jeanette could provide would be a help.

"But I hardly saw him once he finished high school; you can't be interested as far back as that. Yes? You really are? Well, what can I tell you?" Jeanette took another drink. "He did everything right. Whiz kid. Golden boy. Straight A's, and president of any club that counted, and lead in the school play, and then, like I said, the girls. What a show! One managed to fall off her bicycle right in front of our house. She broke her arm, but William noticed her; she accomplished that. And another—Elena Smith, she was in my class—she'd get up an hour early every day and travel clear across town so she could ride to school on the same bus he did; can you imagine?"

Easily. Elena, my sister, my chum, how easily I can imagine your having followed that tenacious and stealthy course. "Couldn't have been so easy to be his sibling," was what she said.

"You're no dope, are you? You look cute, that nose and the silly hair, but you know what's what. Well, if I'd been a boy, maybe you're right, Golden Boy might've been found some night at the bottom of the cellar steps. As it was, a girl, I was in the fan club."

"How about in college?"

"I suppose it was the same. I wouldn't know. I didn't go to college," William's sister said flatly.

She looked up; across the strong square face, a perceptible grimace. "Didn't girls go to—"

"To college forty years ago? Yes, honey, as a matter of fact they did. But not a girl from a lower-middle-class family with two kids if one kid was smarter than the other and there was money for only one."

She had the sense of having turned a corner onto something chillier, darker; she was glad to be able to wait till the bustle of the maid coming in for the tray had played itself out. "How about when William was through college?" she asked then.

"When he was through, anyone could see he was too brainy to go into the little electronics shop that was the family business, so they shipped him off to medical school. And after that," the flat voice added quickly, "they had to pay off the debts, it took years, that college and med school had toted up."

Nan sat silent.

"And then, you want to know? By then I'd married the only man in sight, who was my father's partner in that crummy business. He'd asked me three years running, and by the fourth I figured, well, I'm almost thirty, here I am bookkeeper and receptionist for the business, no chance of anything better turning up—what's your problem?"

Nan hadn't meant for her inquiring eye to be so overt. "I was just—"

"Looking around. I understand. You're thinking this doesn't look like an establishment from the proceeds of a small-time electronics shop. And you haven't seen the half of it. Would you like me to give you a tour? The pool, the gardens?—no, don't be polite. I can see. You're here on business." She finished her drink, the big face wearing its bemused, faintly ironic look. "How did we get this set-up? Good question. How we got it is we came into the money. The business landed a defense contract. One, all anyone needs. It turned out that the machines we used to make some little part of a radio transmitter could also be used to make something indispensable for the communication system of a destroyer. Don't ask how these things happen. You try year after year, you type up forms in quadruplicate, you buy cocktails for some red-faced procurement agent, and then one day it comes through. Bonanza! Bingo!"

Nan put out her hands. "Well, then—"

"D'you want to know why I didn't go to college then? Make something of myself? Listen, honey. By then I was stuck. Married to that man from dullsville. Also, I had a five-year-old child. That's him, our first boy, over there on the mantel. He's your age now. So then I quit work and had another—yes, those pictures—and then a third. Who am I kidding! If that was my chance, I didn't grab it. Maybe your generation does things like that. A college degree for grandma. Toss out the husband you don't like. Start out a new life. Me, I bought this house and settled in for some heavy drinking; that was all the change in the cards for me."

She leaned back, and Nan thought, William again. Just the way he used to sit when he came home tired: broad chin cupped on a fist, mouth slightly open, lids half down over the blue eyes.

"It's the old story, isn't it? One gets rooked so the bright one can shine. Anyhow, he didn't make the choice, our parents did. And you know what? Deep down I don't blame them. You can't help favoring the smart one. I used to watch my boys when they were growing up—which was the William? Well, the answer is, none of them. Not one. Oh, they're all perfectly nice fellows. They remember our birthdays and come for Sunday lunch and tell us what girls they go out with—if we were poor I know damn well they'd pitch in and keep us afloat. But not a spark of talent among them, none. Just three plodding minds that move like their father's, one slow step at a time."

She looked again at the pictures. Not William's talents and not his looks either; in those vacuous faces not a trace of his spacious splendor. "Were you angry at him?" she asked.

"Why would you think that?"

"He said you wouldn't want to come to the wedding."

"Willie said that? My big brother Willie? Listen, honey, what he meant was he wouldn't want us. No, not any arguments; he had his life and we had ours, what's to argue? But William never cared to have us around."

"Maybe he was uncomfortable seeing you."

"Maybe so," Jeanette agreed.

"Maybe he brooded about it so much, about the unfair deal to you, I mean, it seemed a serious mistake."

"Well, now . . ."

She leaned forward, her hands clasped on the table. "Jeanette, listen. He left a letter, a suicide note—I guess they didn't tell you. He said he'd made a mistake. Everyone took for granted it meant me, our marriage, but I was thinking—"

"You were thinking because I got the short end of things forty years ago and screwed up my life, William swallowed those sleeping pills? Well, let me give it to you straight. Sure, I bothered him. Thinking of what little sister pulled down compared to what he did, he must have had some twinges off and on. Stands to reason. He was a decent man; he had a conscience. But he didn't work up the load of guilt you kill yourself for—never, never." The mannish face soberly looked her over. "Sorry, honey. You're a nice kid in a bad spot, and I wish I could help you. The whole thing solved, first crack out of the box. Or I wish you'd take my advice: Go home and enjoy your money and let the whole thing blow over. You won't? You insist on that crackpot scheme? That open-ended stay in a motel so you can go

around asking questions? Okay. In a crazy way maybe I
don't blame you. But don't think it'll be easy; if you want
my opinion, it won't be easy at all."

Chapter
EIGHT

TRAFFIC DOWN TO WASHINGTON WAS LIGHT; it was not quite
four-thirty when she drove into the Sherbourne Arms
Motel, which had been first on Tad's list of recommended
places and which looked promisingly serviceable and drab.
And they had her name: always a good omen. "Mrs. Gardiner? Oh, yes. Room three oh eight. The boys will help
you with your bags."

But Room 308 turned out to be two rooms. Small living
room, good-sized bedroom: a suite. "But I never said—"
Then she stopped. Why not a suite? She was no longer Nan
Dunlop, whose habit of watching pennies had of necessity
been assiduously cultivated. She was a woman whose
money was invested in triple-A bonds, real-estate shelters,
investment trusts—why not a suite? For that open-ended
stay that, as Jeanette had pointed out, would not be easy,
William would want her to have a suite.

Because William was back. During those ugly days after
his death, he had receded, so that sometimes, trying to
reconstruct him, she was shaken by the poverty of the
images she was able to conjure up. What did he look like,
this man who'd plunged her life into such disorder? What

color hair? What kind of voice? But now she had talked to his sister, she was in the city where he did his important work, and he was with her, a presence, confirming her in her decision.

Okay, William dear, I'll keep moving. Five o'clock: plenty of time, I agree, to get in another interview. She washed her face and put on a clean blouse and followed the Exit signs downstairs. Then she stood a second in that indifferent lobby. Her own car, which she had maneuvered into the parking lot in back? No, till she learned her way around Washington's maze of one-way streets and arbitrary prohibitions and elaborately qualified signs, William would want her to take a taxi.

A taxi to get her oriented. Let's see now. South on Wisconsin, past Washington Cathedral, past the Naval Observatory, through the stop-and-go traffic of Georgetown, then a five-minute mess at Wisconsin and M, what if you're really in a rush, then all those no-left-turn signs in a row, then a diagonal, remember that, on Pennsylvania, finally another of those intimidating circles, and we're at the hospital.

An unfamiliar hospital, where instead of breezing in— Hello, Bert, hi, Sally, you too, Dr. Brill—she had to ask at desks, look down rosters of names, walk uncertainly, like a patient, into the elevator. Well, she was a kind of patient, or at least she felt in her stomach a patient's timorous upset. Would he be helpful, this new doctor whom she hadn't called in advance? Would he manage to suggest that the trouble was in some obscure way her own fault? Would he say, Hopeless, young lady, you should have come to me earlier? Or would he not even consent to see her?

Not see her. That seemed obvious. It was five-thirty when she got off at the floor where he had his office; along the hall that had doctors' suites on both sides, the passage of people toward the elevators made clear that the day was over. "Do you have an appointment with Dr. Tyler?" the receptionist asked. "If you don't have an appointment I don't think—"

"Tell him William Gardiner's wife."

"Who?"

"He'll know."

He did know. A short, stout man, he came out right away. Oh, no doubt that he knew; the disapprobation in his small, bright eyes made clear that he knew all he wanted. William's wife, was she? The wife William had married just a month ago? *Two* months, was that so? Well, William had been his dear friend. They hadn't seen each other for many years, but still a dear friend. It had been deeply painful to hear of his death. He was a little surprised to see her, but if she had a problem he'd prefer not to treat her himself; she could understand that, he'd be glad to refer her to—

Then he stopped; he had to stop, because she'd walked out of the reception room, where the receptionist was listening, and into his own office, where he had no choice but to follow. Then she said, "I do have a problem, but it's one that you, people like you, are making."

"I beg your pardon?"

"Dr. Tyler, you heard me right."

"Young lady, we're closing the office; I was about to leave."

"Oh, I can guess what you heard about me. All the details. What someone represented to be the details. Twenty-six-year-old nurse without a penny, and the way those nurses are always out for something, and the whole bag of tricks until she nabbed him, and once she gets him to change his will, the playing around with another man. So then you accept it. All the incriminating symptoms. Well, is that how you practice medicine? Dermatology, that's your specialty, isn't it? So do they tell you the symptoms —the patient has a lesion, a little bleeding, slight discoloration—do you listen and figure you know the story? Without even looking at the case or asking the person most concerned, do you assign it to a standard pattern?"

She was breathless. Think of that. Nan Dunlop, talking like this to a doctor. Talking to him, indeed, the way a nurse in her wildest fantasy doesn't dare to talk to a doctor. Oh, William, William, look what you've brought me to with that terrible deed.

And the doctor took it. At any rate, he didn't throw her out. He shook his head and said that what he heard had been very, um, persuasive.

"I bet it was."

"My dear, won't you sit down?"

"I'm sorry I blew up." But she's not sorry.

"Persuasive," he repeated sadly. "I couldn't conceive that it might not be the truth." He looked older sitting behind his desk; the kind of doctor you go to because your mother did and recommends his experienced sagacity. The cheeks crisscrossed with tiny lines like a road map, the deep furrows running from nostril to chin, the crinkled eyelids: a little old man. I couldn't conceive . . . what he meant, this contemporary of William's, was that he couldn't conceive that anyone who was twenty-six years old might choose *him* for love.

Well, she would not have chosen him, not for a minute. Abruptly, her anger gone, she looked around the office. There were pictures of children in a round frame on his desk, and her gaze lingered on them. "My grandchildren," he said. "Jonathan, Winifred, Mark, Sue. That was a year and a half ago; of course they look different now. Jonathan is a little slow, slow right from the start, poor boy, but otherwise they're all nice children. I guess all children are nice if you treat them right. My dear, I haven't seen William for several years; maybe you'd like to tell me about him."

She did like. She talked and talked, the whole radiant and abbreviated record. She was aware that her account lacked coherence. That is, she went without orderly transition from William's face set with awesome detachment at the hotel desk, to William's voice reverberating across the hospital amphitheater, to William's feet accommodating with easy pleasure to the dance music, to William's laugh booming out across the crowds in his own living room . . . sitting in the chair reserved for patients, she went on and on, while the receptionist stuck her head in to say goodnight, and the phone rang but wasn't answered, and above the court outside the window the sky turned from dusk to dark, and when she finally wound down, he said only, "You've had a grievous loss, haven't you?"

Truce. Better than truce, he believed in her, this little grandfather; he said but of course he'd tell her anything; why yes, right now was as good a time as any, but why him?

"I found your name in his diary."

"So he did keep one. He used to say he would. Well, those were the days. We started here together—I guess you know that. In that era physicians rarely specialized. Do you know that the percentage of physicians who go in for specialization today is four times greater than it was in the thirties —interesting, don't you think? Oh, my dear, you're a nice girl to say so. Anyhow, there we were, William a specialist in pulmonary and cardiac diseases, and me in dermatology, and we went up the ladder together. I'd really like to see the latter years of that diary if it isn't personal."

"It isn't personal at all, but it stops twenty-one years ago."

"Does it? Odd."

Very odd, she didn't say. Disappointing. She had sat last night going over the papers. In this pile of bills, old letters, medical journals, copies of articles written and speeches delivered, in these unsorted layers, would she find a clue? Something to steer her in the right direction?

"Now why would he stop? Twenty-one years ago, let me see. Now that I think of it, that was also the time he curtailed his research. No, he wasn't specific, something to do with limiting damage in heart attacks was all he said. But he was excited. His face lit up when he talked about it, you know that look?—yes, my dear, I guess you do. He said it was one of those simple ideas that could change everything, but he didn't want to talk about it till he did more testing. You have to exercise enormous care in medical research, you know. Those you treat compared with carefully matched controls, methodical checking, caution that nothing harmful is administered—well, William would certainly have been meticulous."

"That simple idea, *did* it change everything?"

"But he quit, as I told you. I said one day how's it going, and he said it was finished. Out the window." The bright eyes blinked kindly at her.

"You mean, the idea didn't work out?"

"That wasn't the way he put it. He just said he wasn't going on."

"But why?"

"No details. Personal reasons forced him to abandon the experiment, was what he said."

Personal reasons: all the factors that can take shelter behind that spacious umbrella. "And you never pressed him to tell you more?"

Dr. Tyler shook a regretful head. Twenty-one years ago he'd been busy himself. It was just around the time his oldest daughter—Winifred and Jonathan's mother, that would be—had become engaged, a very fine young man in the foreign service, but of course that kind of happy event kept them hopping—no, he had not queried William as to his change of plans.

She sat motionless. Maybe he needed money, she said.

"Oh, my dear, one always needs money. But research and a profitable practice don't necessarily preclude each other. Besides, by then he was chief of staff; his reputation was assured; he had enough private patients to set him up."

She was still rigid, hearing the equable timbre of his voice. All those lulling intonations, as if he were saying, we have the lab report here, everything all checked out, so don't worry, my dear, absolutely no malignancy.

However, in this case the malignancy was what she needed; there must be one, she just had to keep probing until she found it. She leaned forward across his desk. "Dr. Tyler, I guess if you and William were so close, you know what he was like. I mean, it was no secret in the hospital that he had, well, a full social life before he married me. Lots of friends, that is. Male and also female. And I wondered if the same had been true for him here in Washington."

The lined face gave a tentative smile and then cut it short, like someone who decides the acquaintance passing on the street is not an acquaintance after all. Yes, William had been a ladies' man. Lots of ladies, no question about it.

"Um hmm. So I thought—it's just an idea—since that faithful record-keeping ended so abruptly, and now you tell me his research also stopped, I thought possibly something troubled him around that time. Some problem with a woman, maybe. Something so, well, unsettling he didn't want to record it; it was preferable just to quit writing."

An error, she could see right away. "That's a serious charge," he said, and there was no smile now to soften the words. How sacrosanct the dead were, and how speedily you could forfeit good will if you appeared to be tarnishing their memory.

"I'm in a serious situation. Dr. Tyler, I don't know if you heard about a note William wrote before he died. A mistake. He'd made a mistake. Well, either he made the mistake in marrying me, in which case I must have been acting in a way calculated to hurt him, or he found out that something he'd inadvertently done many years before had somehow led to someone's suffering, in which case it was his sensitive conscience that was doing the hurting. I can understand how the first hypothesis is an easy one for people to latch on to, but you can see, can't you, that it's the second I really am anxious to prove."

When he turned on the light, the glare illumined his outstretched hands. Had William's hands looked like that, the skin loose and mottled, the veins heavy as if with some secret life of their own? He cleared his throat and coughed and said this wasn't a subject on which he and William had had much discourse. Twenty-one years ago, after all, by then he himself had been married many years—there was that daughter about to be married, well, he'd mentioned her, and a son in college, and another son they were rather distressed about because he proposed to drop out of school and be a forest ranger, but fortunately he got that foolishness out of his system and went back to the classroom where he belonged. So as to William and his, um, love life —another uneasy little cough—it was not a subject on which he considered himself qualified to speak.

So that's it. The subject. His unease wasn't because she maligned the dead but because she brought up sex. William, the ladies' man—how it must have troubled this good friend, this sedate doctor with his three proper children and his wife of long standing so that even now, talking about it, his mouth pursed up and his cough quivered in his throat and his language turned all prim and stilted. Did he try to convert William, offer arguments on the benefits of conjugal felicity? Or did he simply detach himself from that whole unsavory side of his good friend's life? Detach, she thought. When she asked whether he'd ever met any of William's dates, he shook his head. Met them? No, indeed. Highly unlikely. He and Mrs. Tyler would have been pleased to entertain William and anyone he cared to, ah, bring, but things didn't work out that way.

I bet they didn't; leave it to William to discern in which areas he could count on his good friend and in which he couldn't. She looked around the small office. How complicated it was all turning out to be. People talk to me, she had told Tad, and they did, they did; sitting over drinks or staying in their offices well past closing time, they talked their hearts out. But what they talked about was not the William whose newly defined past would exonerate her, but the one who reflected their own problems and predilections. Me, me, me, a lengthy and indirect disclosure.

"In any case, you're right, he did have a sensitive conscience," Dr. Tyler unexpectedly said, and she understood it was a sop, compensation for the reports on sexual matters he wouldn't or couldn't bring himself to confide.

She'd been getting ready to leave, but she settled back again.

"Of course I was never in any doubt about his sensitivity, but I saw it in full force when he was obliged to write an unfavorable report about a resident."

"Goodness, when was this?"

"Actually, around the time we were talking about before. I remember because he called one evening to say that he had something to discuss, and right after that my daughter called about this nice young man she wanted us to meet.

The engagement was announced in June, and naturally she introduced Larry to us well before that, let's say late March or early April, and that would work out right because April is when we turn in the annual ratings for the residents in our department."

"An unfavorable report—is it so unusual?"

"It'd better be unusual," he said with his cheerful pedantry. "When you think of the checking we do before we take them: marks, recommendations, family, ethnic background —those young doctors are screened to within an inch of their lives. But of course we're not unfallible; once in a while we pick a lemon and we have to say so."

"Only William didn't like saying so?"

"My dear, it's never easy. Not for any of us. If there were standardized tests, as there are in some professions. But though the National Board of Examiners did devise one several years ago—well, you're not interested in that. At any rate, there it is, those young men and women, how do you rate their intellect, how do you rate their medical capabilities, how do you rate their character? Excellent, good, or fair—which? An assignment to draw on all one's powers of thoughtfulness and discrimination."

Nan sat silent. She usually heard the other side of it. That bastard, I work my ass off, cover up for him when he's drunk, make the right assessment twice as often as he does, and he gives me a lousy "good." She asked if Dr. Tyler remembered the problem with the resident in William's case.

"I can't forget it. Seemed nothing wrong with the intellectual faculty; the fellow was damn bright. And surely nothing with the medical; he was a crackerjack tactician, meticulous at making a diagnosis or revising a hypothesis."

"Well, then?"

"The character," he said portentously. "That attribute

that's not susceptible to being pinned down. Even William couldn't do it. I tried to help him. Was it a moral fault? An ethical one? You know William, usually so articulate. But not this time. Finally he blurted out—how well I remember—the fellow's bad medicine. He has a nasty acquisitive streak. He's the kind that gives specialists a bad name."

"Is that what he put in the report? Nasty acquisitive streak?"

"I don't know what he finally wrote. I only know what he came to me for—to find some euphemistic phrasing that would make the point and at the same time evade the worst of the offensiveness." Dr. Tyler fixed her with his gentle stare. "There is no such euphemism, of course; William knew it. Take it from me, my dear, when William got through with that report, Dr. X did not come out smelling very good."

"What happens to someone who gets that kind of rating?"

"He's finished, of course. His career demolished." The veined hands turned slowly over. "Oh, possibly he can get a post in general medicine at some backwater hospital. Some of those southern states are so poor they have no choice; they'll take anyone. But as for his continuing in his chosen specialty, or getting into a prestigious hospital like this one, not a chance."

"So he's a ruined man, you might say?"

"I think anyone would say."

She looked for a second at the wing opposite this one. A nurse was stripping a bed; she could see the agile hands forming the ungainly bundle out of the soiled sheets. "Dr. Tyler, it might be really important for me to know who that disqualified resident was. So if you could make it possible for me to see those records."

But she knew before she'd finished speaking, the jolt of

the neat gray head and the quiver of the lined cheeks made it clear: viewing confidential reports, oh, my dear, pernicious in its way as having extramarital sex. She said thank you and stood up. If she was going to find him, this undesirable doctor whose career William had ruined, it wouldn't be through the helpfulness of William's erstwhile colleague.

Chapter
NINE

THERE WERE FLOWERS AT THE MOTEL when she came back: a fall bouquet whose pinks and reds and rusts and blazing oranges asserted themselves with robust cheeriness against the pallid walls. Her spirits lifted; she guessed the donor before she'd even poked around to find the card. Then she made the phone call.

"Tad, thanks. They made my day."

"So you got here."

"Just this afternoon."

"I beat you by a day. I've been calling to see when you'd check in."

"I was going to call you anyhow." Then quickly, lest he get the wrong idea: "I need a favor."

Good, he said, they'd have lunch tomorrow. Then he stopped, that meaningful pause, and it all came back. Watch it. Presumed guilty. Here as in New York, people ready to misinterpret . . . all the strictures that proscribe any casual meeting place, interject into friendship just the element of furtiveness it doesn't need.

He was more adept at handling it than she was. "Nan, I have to show up at some conference tomorrow morning at the Hilton. Even a newcomer like you knows where that is, and there's this little restaurant across the street so I could scoot right over—got a pencil?"

She had a pencil. Trust Tad to turn adversity into expedience, pretend the awkward arrangement is for their dual convenience. And it was in fact convenient. The little restaurant turned out to be big on kinky decoration: lavender and black walls, sinuous murals, determinedly insufficient light: an atmosphere of earnest seduction in a place where you settled down for lentil soup and chef's salad. But it was across from the hotel and three down from the corner as promised, and he was there when she arrived, the familiar face and agreeable smile. A boon. Someone for whom it was not necessary to turn on either the pat defensiveness or the bellicose resolve; she could be herself, which at this point was troubled and uncertain and awed at the magnitude of her task. She didn't even have to talk immediately about that task; as they looked at each other across the small black table she could chatter on about cars and traffic as if she were just any tourist come to the nation's capital for a spot of sight-seeing: ". . . So I resolved I would master that drive, motel to hospital, such a snap in a taxi, but dear lord, those one-way signs—is it true they change them every half hour to test your patriotism? And the traffic circles; if you aren't sure exactly which exit to turn off at, every truck in Washington lets you know you're fouling up their schedule."

But of course she couldn't chatter on, Tad was the one, indulgent but firm, to remind her. "Nan, is this whole thing going to be too much for you?"

She took a breath. "Yes. I mean no. That is, I started already. Yesterday on the way down I stopped to see William's sister, interesting but I'll tell you another time, and late yesterday afternoon I saw Dr. Tyler."

"The dermatologist?"

"He was one of William's good friends; I found his name in the diary."

"Ah. The diary that is going to unlock all the secrets."

"Well, not quite, I'm afraid. It's a very businesslike affair. Who he saw, highlights of important cases, summaries of meetings, notes on professional reading. You're in it, incidentally. Lunch with new residents, Tad Collins and Mitchell Stone."

"Several lunches," he said with the strained smile that always accompanied his mention of William.

"Anyhow, this great jumble of names and medical data, but nothing personal, no judgments at all, to help me. Except there is something that may be helpful. It ends twenty-one years ago. First he's so faithful, every day itemized, his professional life you might say intact, and then nothing. Just a last notation in the middle of a page. Also, that's the time, Dr. Tyler told me, he dropped his research."

"Research on what?"

"William hadn't got around to telling him. He just said there was some idea, one of those inspired intuitions, William was all steamed up about it, and then poof, finished. So my idea is that something happened around then to really shake him, and that's why he quit."

Tad waited while the waitress laid out their order on the inadequate table. Then he said, "Twenty-one years ago. He was wildly busy. He'd recently been made chief of staff, and he had his private practice, and then the teaching. To say nothing of the personal life he didn't record for posterity. And a diary is implacable. Like a child. Worse than a child. Maybe he decided those relentless demands weren't worth it."

She put down her spoon; the lentil soup was a disappointment. "Tad, look. I have to do this one small step at a time. I mean, if I can't limit it, work along the lines of a single theory, then the whole thing really will be, as you say, too much. So this is my limit for now. That period when the diary stops. If it doesn't work, I'll figure out something else." She heard her voice—please agree, play along, I need bolstering—and he nodded, that understanding Tad; it does make sense; by all means stick with it, and what about Dr. Tyler?

"Well, we'd been speculating, you and I, about a woman. Someone he hurt. I could see her, that misled girl, with her thwarted life. But Dr. Tyler mentioned a resident, someone to whom William gave an unfavorable evaluation, and it got me thinking along a different line."

"If you're talking twenty-one years back, that would have been my year."

"Well, it can't be you"—her little stab at levity—"because you were taken on the staff, and I don't need anyone to tell me that honor goes to only the top drawer. Anyhow, I thought, I hoped, you'd help me take a look at them. William's evaluations, I mean. Oh, don't say it. I know those things are strictly confidential, but they must be filed someplace, and since you agree how important . . ." Did he agree? She sat looking at the wall bracket in the shape of a flower that curved up from the lavender wall.

"You really think for twenty-one years William cherished the idea of this young man whose career he ruined, and he decided he'd been too harsh, and the idea so distressed him he committed suicide?"

Will it always be like this, first the wild elation clutching at her ribs, and then the reversal, the sense of something sagging inside her, as logic coldly shows up the frailty of her idea?

But now Tad swung around. "Actually, there may be something to it. Suppose that miserable fellow hurt someone else, and he or she in turn went haywire, a whole chain of catastrophe because of one harsh rating, oh, I think you should look into it; you have to look into everything."

That doggedly hearty tone—he didn't really believe it. Well, all the more decent of him to string along if he didn't really believe it, and besides, it was true; she did have to look into everything. She murmured thanks and reached out to put her hand on his, and at the same instant a shadow from above fell on them.

Trapped. She'd known without looking whose card would be tucked in with the flowers at the motel, and with the same abrupt insight she now knew whose face would be glaring down at their intertwined hands. Maybe it's the cruelest trick life can play, she thought, to put you in the spot where you know you're innocent but you look guilty, and you can't protest your innocence because protestations would only make things worse; all you can do is brazen it out while the pain of injustice burns behind your eyes and scratches like paper in your throat.

She brazened it out. "Hello, Victor." She was about to add, Do you know Dr. Collins, but of course he knows Dr. Collins; they've already gone through the travesty of courteous greeting and mandatory handshake.

Another handshake now; Tad engineered it. Tad was the only one able to engineer anything. She sat slumped, bent over the wilted lettuce they utilized for chef's salad here, and as for Victor, after the first intercepted glance, his caustic gaze went around the restaurant, as if to find in its dim lighting and tawdry decor the reason for their having selected it.

He could, however, talk: one up on her. When Tad said such a surprise, seeing him here, he said not so surprising at all; he often came to Washington on business and stayed across the street.

"Convenient," Tad said.

"Very," Victor answered.

"Near everything," Tad said.

"Certainly is," Victor assented.

Oh, God, were they going to go on like this, as if it were just any of the little coincidental meetings that took place every day in the vicinity of Connecticut Avenue and T Street? Yes, with the waitress having to walk around them and light from the flowerlike fixture bisecting Victor's face, they were going to go on like this. Tad said, "Warm for this time of year," and Victor said, "Sometimes in November," and Tad said, "But no more colors in Rock Creek Park," and Victor said, "Unfortunately, no," and Tad said, "Spring is really the time in Washington," and Victor said, "How long do you plan to stay here?"

Then he said it again, "How long do you plan to stay here," and the realization stirred: He was talking to her, the stupefied one, the zombie.

How long? Till I find out the truth about William. Till I have sufficient proof to take that look of threatening insolence off your face. "Oh, well, I'm not sure. I mean . . ."

"Interesting town," Victor said. "Well, enjoy yourself," he said. "Have to go now," he mercifully said, and did. With his face set, he made his way between the tables and out the door.

"Still hostile," Tad lightly said.

"God, yes." Didn't he understand the implications for her of this fortuitous meeting? Evidently not. Sweet Tad. *Innocent* Tad, because all he said was it seems funny; if Victor was planning to meet someone here in the restaurant, he certainly didn't seem to look for them. She pushed aside her plate. "He wasn't meeting anyone, he had no plans to. He has second sight, that man. He was walking by, and some divination told him he'd find me here in just the kind of incriminating circumstance he likes to find me, so that's the reason he came in, and now he's happy; all his nasty suspicions are confirmed."

"Nan, take it easy."

"True. He hates me. He has to hate me. He loved William, I'm just beginning to realize how close they were. One of those alliances between people of different age, different outlook, but it works. I mean, a doctor and a lawyer, there's usually no great common interest. But this was better. It was a case of attracting personalities. William admired him, that tight intellect, all tension and industry, but he could turn it off when the child was around; he could be the classic, loving, worried-sick father. And Victor, well, Victor found William's expansiveness fascinating, I understand that now—that the distinguished doctor, someone who was usually uptight and dignified, that he could go dancing and take out girls and not give a hoot about his position. But then he took out the wrong girl, me, and I managed to do him in. And Victor in some meaningful way has to retaliate, since the police seem unable to do the job he's appointed himself chief retaliatory agent." She quieted down. "Tad, I'm okay. Don't worry."

He was worrying. It was obvious in the look of solicitude on his pleasant features. Solicitude, not sex. Their relationship was changed; she understood that; it was clear from the moment she saw him waiting for her at the door of the restaurant. The sexual spark was missing. That man who had to exercise extravagant control to keep from caressing her when they came home in a taxi, who fought to hold down his desire, who quivered when their hands came for

a second into accidental conjunction—gone, gone, the mandate of circumstance had erased him. That was why the full
horror of Victor's appearance didn't hit him, because he
himself was so far from feeling what Victor imputed to
him.

Oh, Victor, you vindictive fool. There was nothing between Tad and me before, and there's even less now. He
doesn't in the least desire me. I'm a cause. His own private
particular cause. A man doesn't want to go to bed with a
cause. I arouse in him protectiveness but not passion; solicitude has wiped out lust. That's why he can sit here showing
me all this kindness, because kindness is all he feels.

"Eat your salad," Tad told her. That gently caring tone
—like a brother, an uncle.

"I'm not hungry."

"We can order something else if—"

"Tad, can we go to look at those records now?"

"Now? This minute?"

"Would you mind terribly? Of course if you want des-
sert. Or you don't have time."

She saw him hesitate again, the kindly uncle. If he were
still in love with her, he would have the will to say no. No
is obviously the reasonable thing to say. You don't just drop
everything, mess up schedules, go shooting off in response
to a crack-brained scheme; you say, well, how about four-
thirty Wednesday.

But because he's not remotely in love with her, he feels
duty bound to help her, and he says, "All right, just let me
make a phone call to tell someone I'll be late and I'll see if
I can swing it at the hospital."

He did swing it. A quick taxi ride, a few words to charm
the elderly woman who presided over the files in a remote
room tucked in with the second-floor offices, and Tad was
handing her a couple of manila folders. "They'll be in

there. The year you want, the year before, the year after. Should be three or maybe four entries for each." He paused, his hand on the table where she was sitting. "Including mine. I know William said complimentary things about me; none of this is exactly secret, but I'd just as soon not be around while you read it."

With that, discreetly, he went to the other side of the room, and she was alone with William. William's clear handwriting. William's palpable sense of pleasure. William's exuberant style. "Excellent, good, fair," Dr. Tyler had said, and it was within these stilted categories that he probably did keep the evaluations of his own residents, but not William. Never her William. On the long sheets designed for formal appraisals, he managed to give each young man or woman a jovial pat on the back. "Any department of pulmonary medicine will be damn lucky to get Helen Moss." "Mitchell Stone has an intuitive sense that makes him a whiz in the sickroom." "For three years, Bruce Whitticomb has carried the load in this department." And, as Tad had diffidently suggested, "Thadeus Collins, first-rate doctor."

Well, but what about the one he had decided not to pat on the back? The one with a mean acquisitive streak? She went through the folder again: intuitive sense . . . carried the load . . . first-rate . . . lucky. Maybe in her fervor she was going too fast, letting pages stick together or projecting her own thoughts onto that plain-dealing handwriting. All right, slowly now: Stone, Whitticomb, Collins, Moss. Then the year after. The year before.

". . . so Dr. London and I both went in, we looked at the chart together": Tad at the other end of the room, charming that elderly matron so she, Nan, can take her time, keep looking until she finds it.

She laid the pages fanwise on the table. Errors are made

in a hospital—who that's ever worked in one doesn't know it. The wrong patient is wheeled down to X-ray. The diabetic doesn't get his insulin. A bit of thread is left inside the incision. A healthy organ is removed. Devastating errors, but, in a manner of speaking, honest ones. Accident and not intent is to blame; while the results may be lethal, the perpetrators are without purpose. Carelessness, boredom, strain, fatigue—these and not ill will are the culprits.

Could the missing evaluation be put into that inadvertent category? Or was some more meaningful factor at work, so Dr. X didn't turn up here in the company of his worthy colleagues?

She put the papers into the folder and went across the room, where Tad was still offering judicious reminiscence, and the woman was responding with demure approbation. "Find what you were after?"

"Oh, yes. Thanks very much."

She waited till she and Tad were halfway down the hall; then she turned. "He's not there."

"What d'you mean?"

"The one William thought was rotten. Booted out."

He stood against the frosted glass pane in a door. Room 205, said the gold letters: Enter through Room 211. "William was his own man; he wouldn't be pinned down to a rigid system of ratings. Maybe you missed it."

"No chance."

"Or maybe Frank Tyler was wrong about the year."

"It coincided with his daughter's engagement; someone like Dr. Tyler doesn't make a mistake about the time his oldest daughter gets engaged. Besides, you gave me other years; I looked through them all. Once he said someone would function better as an internist than specializing, but that was as far in deprecation as he ever went."

"Maybe Tyler was wrong about the whole incident."

"Curious thing to be wrong about," she said.

"Or maybe William changed his mind—no, of course not; about a thing like that I realize he wouldn't." He was silent while a man walked behind them, rattled the door handle of 205, and with a groan moved down the hall to 211. "Beats me," Tad finally said.

She shifted her pocketbook to the other shoulder. "Well, anyhow, one good thing. I found something in his hand-writing. No, not an evaluation—just some medical notes that must have slipped in by accident."

"Let's see."

"That woman—if she knew I snitched something out of her precious folders. William's handwriting, don't you agree? As if I could mistake it. Anything of William's, no reason I should leave them, is there?"

"No reason at all," Tad said as he handed back the crumpled pieces of paper.

"I'm glad to have them, any extra scrap to go in the collection, but oh God, how I'd give them up for something definite. That evaluation."

Tad ran his fingers through his hair. "Nan, I'm sorry."

"It's all right."

"All your hopes, you were going to find something here. Finale to quest."

"Some quest, to end on its second day," she said lightly.

"Why not? You deserve it. You've been through unjust torment; why shouldn't you run into unexpected triumph?"

She saw the concern on his face. Too much concern; it reminded her again that she had gone from love object to worthy cause. Oh, she didn't blame him for no longer finding her desirable. Logic decreed the change, William's death decreed it, the whole set of bizarre circumstances decreed it. In fact, if he did try to make love to her, if his hand went out to caress her in the old suggestive way, she would indignantly reject it. It would offend everything, all the memories and experiences, they had in common.

But still, there was that vague regret: vanity exercising its rights over reasonableness. In a sense, it was another rejection, at a time when she'd amassed her quota. The worthy cause stood very straight. "Tad, you've been wonderful, I really appreciate it. But don't worry about me. I'm not exactly a bereft woman, don't forget. I have plenty of money; I know my way around; I can work at this indefinitely." Another man tried the door and with the same disgruntled mumbling went down the hall. She said okay, a dead end here, but she could have ten dead ends and still come up with something. What she would do now was go back to her first idea. Some woman. And right here in the hospital—no, thanks, for this she didn't need Tad's help— was surely the place to start.

That dogged optimism was the right tack. He murmured something about her being an okay girl, gave her hand the platonic clasp that springs from fervent relief, and then, walking at a good clip down the hall, was off: man escaping from a predicament that has proved itself impervious to his powers.

Chapter
TEN

SHE KNEW HER WAY AROUND, she'd told Tad, and it was true. Even here, this hospital where she'd been only once before. Different names and faces from her own hospital, but, she felt sure, similar bureaucratic alignments, similar authorities keeping peremptory eyes over zealously held domains. Like going into a branch of one's own supermarket, and knowing, oh, joy, where everything is: down this aisle the tuna, on that bottom shelf the cream of mushroom, in this alcove the only brand of marmalade worth eating—no waste motion, none of that nervous fumbling that makes you decide you don't want the marmalade after all.

Here in Northwest Memorial, no waste motion now. It was two-thirty when she consulted with a white-haired man in Personnel, and he kindly sent her, well before three, to someone across the hall—Yes, that door, dear—who was not so old but also rather less sympathetic, and he with palpable unease but punctilious accuracy sent her to a room on the third floor, turn left, second door on the right, and due to the instructions she received here, by half past three she was at her destination, which was a Miss Hope Emory who twenty-one years ago had been head nurse on Five Cavendish, where William had his patients, but who, having failed to rise in the profession, had come

so far down in it as to be office nurse for a neurological
group that had offices in a wing across the street.

Miss Emory was not reluctant to talk. "Dr. Gardiner?
Yes, of course I remember. That frenzy when he came on
the floor; even if you didn't see him, one look at the nurses
would tell you he was there. They'd dart into the lounge
and come out with fresh lipstick; they'd cancel lunch dates;
they'd find some good reason why they had to leave their
patients and walk down the hall to the linen room. Demor-
alizing. You run an efficient floor, and then an attractive
doctor comes along and they're twittering schoolgirls."

Miss Emory was not attractive, and must have been less
so twenty years ago; now at least the sharp features and
jutting chin could seem the concomitant of shrewdness and
experience. "And they meddle with schedules. I guess
that's the most discreditable," she said in her aggrieved
voice, as if she were still having to cope with those un-
worthy tactics. "You have it all set up, who's to cover the
post-op cases, who handles the terminal patients, who takes
around medications, and then bam. Your most reliable
nurse asks to switch her hours because there's a crisis at
home; only look closely and the crisis turns out to be a need
to show up at the nurses' station at half past one, which is
when the doctor looks at charts. Can you believe professional women will stoop to such strategems?"

Nan nodded. Yes, she could believe.

Miss Emory answered the phone. No, Dr. Thomas
wasn't in; none of the doctors was in at present, but if the
patient wished to leave his name. Then she drew herself up:
back to William. "Of course in such cases the man himself
isn't exempt from blame. If he didn't show himself as willing to accept such overtures, the overtures would not be
made. However, you tell me he's dead; perhaps we should
not speak ill of the dead in this office."

Nan's chair squeaked when she leaned back, muffling her involuntary moan. Then she cleared her throat and said did Miss Emory by any chance know if any of the young nurses actually went out with Dr. Gardiner.

"Of course I know; if you're head nurse you know everything. Because you're a few years older, they think you're ancient. Hope Emory, over the hill. They whisper right in front of you, as if you're incapable of understanding their hysterical shorthand. But you understand it all; if you want to do your job you'd better understand."

Couldn't have done her job so well, Nan thought, if she's now reduced to saying, No, Dr. Thomas isn't in; Dr. Shearson isn't in either. She sent a conciliatory smile across the desk and said did Miss Emory remember the names of the nurses who went out with Dr. Gardiner.

"I remember what I told them," she said through tight lips. "He'd never marry them, never never. But they don't listen, those young girls. They go on deluding themselves. Excuse me, you're not so old yourself. Well, take it from me, don't get mixed up with a doctor."

Nan sat silent while Miss Emory told someone else, or perhaps the same person, Dr. Thomas wasn't in.

"Nurse and doctor, it doesn't work, it can't; it ends the way it ended for those two."

Try again. "Which two?"

Miss Emory's eyes were fixed on her. "Why'd you say you were asking all this?"

She moved forward in the squeaking chair and proffered the explanation she'd told Tad would serve for those whom the truth might deter: doing research for someone who's writing a book on Dr. Gardiner.

"Believe me, the messes those two girls made of their own lives, they'd be no help to you at all."

"I'd still like to speak to anyone who—"

"For nurses who are presumed to have made a study of the workings of mind and body, for them to be so foolhardy—"

"Miss Emory, it would really be a help to know their names."

"It's so long ago; actually, I don't even remember."

Nan sat a moment. Piled up next to her were the charts Miss Emory was filing. Havemeyer, John: trigeminal neuralgia, read the top one. "Dr. Collins is very interested in this project," Nan said. "Dr. Thadeus Collins, maybe you remember him. He said to me, see Hope Emory; if there's anything to know about that period, she knows it."

Miss Emory raised the jutting chin. She moved Havemeyer, John under Heller, E. She looked at the silent phone. Then she said, "Gail Walsh and Marcy Drummond."

"I see. And what kind of messes did they get into?"

"All I can tell you is, I wouldn't care to leave a hospital under the circumstances they did. First Gail," she said with bitter satisfaction, "then Marcy."

"If you could give me an idea of the circumstances . . ." But she'd had her allotment; she could see from the expression on the woman's face that she'd had more than her rightful allotment. Miss Emory folded her hands and said she wasn't authorized to say any more. Miss Dunlop could of course speak to those unfortunate women herself, for all the good it would probably do her. Their addresses? It wasn't for her to say even if she knew, which she didn't; Personnel would be the ones to tell her that.

Personnel, after some small persuasion, did tell her, but by then it was after five, and she went back to the drab comfort of the Sherbourne Arms Motel. Back to its restaurant, which turned out to be decorated with ships' lanterns and nautical placemats, and then to the rooms designed for orderly living and sound sleeping. Except she didn't sleep well; sometime after one she roused herself from fitful nightmare and went to the window, where in the dim light across the street she saw a car with a man looking out. She stood unmoving behind the thin curtain. Lots of reasons why a man at quarter past one might stand at the side entrance of a motel. He's just driven in from out of town. He's waiting for someone who will shortly come out. He thought he heard a funny noise in the engine. But he wouldn't just park there, would he? After five minutes, ten, he would drive on. And that long slender face, barely visible in the light from the corner—there must be dozens of men with faces of that particular configuration; because Victor's face is shaped like that is no proof of anything. Anyhow, why should it be Victor? Even if he went to the trouble of calling every hotel in Washington until he discovered the one where she's staying, why should he park outside her window; what would be the purpose?

The car edged forward and then, slowly, back. Maybe he wants to know if Tad is here. She might yell out this third-floor window: All right, come on in and check it out; you'll see, I'm alone, no one with me in bed. But she was not geared for yelling out of hotel windows at night, and besides, now she pulled the curtain aside, it might be just a trick of light that imparted to the thin face the intimation of menace she'd read in the restaurant that afternoon, and besides, now he was driving away; the car went forward again and this time kept going.

Back to her solitary bed. Okay, suppose it was Victor. A Victor driven by malice and obsessed curiosity. There is no way he can hurt her, none. In fact, now her investigation's on track, she's in a position to hurt him, or at least to undermine the powers of reasoning he's so proud of. If the leads with Gail and Marcy work out as it's logical to expect they will, she'll be possessed of the proof to show up that brilliant lawyer, and the idea instilled such confidence that in the morning she maneuvered her own car out of the parking lot and drove to the address in southwest Washington where Personnel had told her Gail Walsh now lived.

How will it be with this woman out of William's past? First impressions are what counts: every nurse's tenet. You walk in, and you either win over the patient, so he's willing to believe your ministrations will make the difference, or you so antagonize him that hours of dedicated nursing fail of their full effect. She'd antagonized Miss Emory, she knew that; something in her manner or message had struck that parched woman wrong, so she had played it close to her chest, kept back by old grievance or new irritation from disclosing all she knew.

Well, she'd better not antagonize Gail Walsh, who is now Mrs. Ralph Hudak. Mrs. Hudak, I'm doing research for a book about Dr. William Gardiner, he died last month, I wonder if you remember him. . . . she rehearsed it as she went up in the self-service elevator, and again walking down the long hall, and again as she stood in front of the door which was the replica of a dozen other doors in this barrackslike apartment. Then the woman appeared and she said it again. "Mrs. Hudak, I'm doing research . . ."

No antagonism here, just a flustered surprise. "William Gardiner dead, think of that. That beautiful hulk of man, he was my first love. There's something about the first; I don't care who comes after; you never get over that thrill when he looks over the field and it's you he picks."

You could see why he picked her. Or, at least, you could visualize what had been the lures of twenty years before to make him pick her. Will I change like that, Nan thought, my pretty breasts all sagging, my upper arms rippling with fat, my waist so thick that the skirt zipper won't close? And will I keep fussing with my looks, first tugging at the zipper, then pulling down a blouse, then going over to the mirror to add lipstick to an already painted bottom lip? Nan sat in the designated chair. Morbid. That's what this whole business was making her.

Gail bent to brush off her shoes and asked how come anyone gave her name.

"I got it from Miss Emory at the hospital. First I went to the Nursing Supervisor's office, and they sent me to Records, and they told me Miss Emory ran the fifth floor at the time I'm interested in."

"Ran it! She held it in her hot little hand." Gail tugged again at the zipper but no use. "If you didn't tuck in a sheet properly at one end of the hall, a mark showed up in Hope Emory's black book at the other end. What's she like now?"

"She sounded angry, actually."

"Look, do you want a cup of coffee? Tea? You don't mind if I do, do you? The day I have ahead, I really need it. So old Emory was pissed off. You can't blame her, really. William took her dancing once. No, twice; he really did. She was a good dancer; it was the only thing she cared about aside from making our lives miserable. Sure you don't want coffee?"

"Maybe I will, thanks."

"Decaf. The only kind Ralph allows in the house. He says caffeine injures the brain cells. Sugar? Cream? Well, old Emory, William took her out twice, but that was it. Next thing anyone knew, we were a thing, him and me, and Emory found out; she found out everything, and naturally it riled her. She never forgave him."

So that explains it: not any tactlessness on her part, but the predilection for cute looks on William's—the sexual offense that can hold its grudge through two decades. Nan drank the coffee and braced herself for the inevitable next

question: How did that darling William die? Would there
be tears? Heavy sentiment? Would the questions be insistent, so she'd have to dissemble about the suicide she'd
resolved not to mention? But Gail seemed more interested
in the sweep of her hair than in grief for a first love; she
stood in front of the mirror and said so he was dead, that
gorgeous man; well, they none of them had it easy.

Nan put down her cup. The messes those two young
women made of their lives, Miss Emory had said, but no
messed-up life was apparent here. A pleasant enough living
room, undistinguished, with definite signs of children:
school books piled on the table, a book bag on the floor, a
sweater with the letter S tossed on the couch. On the other
hand, Gail did seem rattled about something—all those
trips to the mirror to put on lipstick, take off lipstick, re-
arrange her hair.

Nan spoke carefully. "I know it's personal, but Miss
Emory said something about your having left the hospital
under, well, unhappy circumstances."

"I bet she said worse than that. It wasn't exactly private.
I was four months pregnant—everyone knew, why
shouldn't she tell you?" Working on her hair now, drawing
a comb down again and again to get the part exactly
straight. "You think it's funny, I bet. A nurse right there
in the hospital doing nothing about it when she gets herself
knocked up. But that was twenty-one years ago, we didn't
run so fast to abortions then. Anyhow, Washington's a
small town, really; no one thinks it, but we have small-town
ways. And anyhow . . ." She paused: a little more lipstick
on the top lip. "Anyhow, you always have these dreamy
ideas about what's going to happen. How a man will look
at you, and think, Oh, glory, his child, and inside him
something will click. Even if he told you honestly beforehand he wasn't fixing to get married, inside him something

will click. Well, I was younger then; I believed in romance." She combed her hair forward and then tied it back. "So what did happen, I had the baby and Ralph married me."

Her gestures were more frenzied; another dab at her hair, then she pulled over it a brimmed hat. "How do I look?"

Nan hesitated.

"Go on, you can say it. Not so good. This hat's a wreck; I used to wear it in the rain. But they say you should wear a hat; it makes you look dignified. Dignified and motherly, what they're after; they say that's how you can do him the most good."

They? Him? She must have looked her bafflement; the fluttering movements stopped for a second. "I didn't tell you. It's Leland. He's being arraigned this morning. Ten o'clock. They say he broke into this liquor store last night, and this morning is his arraignment."

"Leland?"

"I thought things were getting better. No trouble for five whole months. I said to Ralph, he's working at that job, now he's turned twenty; wait and see, he'll change for the better. And then they called me last night. What do you think? A scarf or not?"

Nan still couldn't talk. Leland—even about the name she'd been romantic, this woman who knew beforehand the father wasn't fixing to marry her. So a stepfather named Ralph was all the father a boy ever knew, and last night he got in trouble again, and this morning was his day in court. Oh, Gail, forgive me. I thought you were just a dumb housewife worried about your hair style. I put you down for empty-headed. And here you are going off to show the authorities your son has motherliness and strength behind him; if it were me I'd be having hysterics.

She spoke at last. "Listen. I have a car outside. I can drive you if you like."

"Oh, hey, that would be—if you sure you don't—maybe I'll wear the scarf, no, I—well, maybe this one." She did wear it. Or, rather, she clutched it, clutched the tan striped scarf, her black gloves, her pocketbook, and some papers as she sat upright in the car. "It's Indiana Avenue, the courthouse, you know where that is? I'll show you where to turn. They say it matters if the mother comes; it shows there's a supportive family behind him; the judge takes that into consideration when he—I don't know. Last time didn't matter at all. I was right there, this new black suit, and it didn't help in the least; they wouldn't give him bail, and once you don't get bail it's a sure thing your sentence will be longer because they take for granted—maybe you ought to turn here. Right on K, and then try Fourth."

She did try Fourth, while the woman beside her put on gloves and took them off. "A father sitting there would help too, I asked Ralph this morning. If he'd just come and sit. Well, you can't blame him for not. A kid who's been trouble ever since he's ten years old, a man gets discouraged; it's only natural. And Ralph tried in the beginning; he really did. It's just their being so different. Incompatible, you have to call it. Ralph is big on sports and all; there isn't a better phys ed teacher in the District. And his own two kids take after him. Steve, he's captain of the swimming team in high school, and he makes good money working in this sporting goods store after school. And Caroline plays girls' hockey every afternoon, some team that takes the best from all the high schools. No left turn, it says there, you better go on another block." She had the scarf wrapped around a finger; she was chewing on it. "It wasn't that Leland was dumb. I remember when he was in fourth grade or was it fifth, his teacher told me, that boy's going to be a real little whiz at math. But Ralph saw it different. What team you trying out for, Ralph would say. Get off your butt and go outside; you'll feel better, Ralph would say. And there would be Leland, working at some puzzle, five hundred pieces, he could do it like a shot. Yes, incompatible from the word go, you have to say it. It's that building there, the one with all that glass. Want to come in? You don't have to."

She very much didn't want to come in. She didn't want to park, or get out of the car, or join that desultory crowd going in under the arched doorway, all the women clutching hats and gloves and pocketbooks in that effort to embody the attributes of motherliness and dignity that might induce a judge to go easy on their erring sons. But this was what she had come for, wasn't it? The end of the line—it might well be here, in this building where the crowds stood around talking, or drinking coffee, or lined up at the phone booths, or just posed for interminable waiting—people geared for the worst. Besides, Gail needed her; the euphoric flutters were gone; there was only a wide-eyed pallor as they looked up their room on the printed schedule hanging on a wall. The brimmed hat slipped sideways, and she straightened it. How do I look, she said, but what she meant now was don't go away, stay with me, help me face it. Nan nodded; of course she was going to stay; in a minute she would see him, the personification of a man's mistake.

They sat in the second row, and she could tell right away that Leland was there, one of the dozen or so on the long bench up front, because Gail stiffened, and then looked resolutely away, and then, from under the insistent brim, assayed another look, and then with a little sob stared down at her lap. "That's him," she whispered. "Third one."

Third from left—she would never have known. That boy with the sallow skin, slicked-back hair, round passive face

—nothing familiar. Did he see his mother come in? He must have; his gaze went over them. But no change in his expression, no hint of recognition in the shaded eyes, not a twitch of the tight mouth.

Well, his expression is not supposed to change. His mother is there to lend his case support, but there's no mechanism at this point for her to talk to him, not even a prescribed way to wave or smile. She can only sit, like the others scattered around, with sorrowing apprehension, while in that inaccessible section separated from them by just a few feet, he aims for bravado and impassivity.

"Take off your jacket. This can take hours," Gail said. And in fact well over an hour went by before Leland was called. First there was a disheveled man who on the whispered advice of counsel pleaded guilty to criminal trespass, and then three prostitutes, all drawing the same sentence, conditional discharge, and walking out with the same look of sheepish defiance, and then a boy whose family must be in the row behind because they all let out a sigh—mother, father, baby, sister, brothers—when he was released on his own recognizance, and then a long interval so the court reporter could leave the room, and then a woman who after stabbing her husband had taken him to the hospital—she sat right there, your honor, while they stitched him up, five children at home, your honor—but his honor, unmoved, set two thousand dollars bail.

"Where in God's name can that woman get two thousand dollars?" Nan whispered, but there was no answer because the court officer was calling off a number, and it was Leland up there in front of the judge, and suddenly everything was hushed.

A new air of concentrated stillness: with Leland's case, something was going on. This wasn't just the routine of a girl picked up on a street corner, back three weeks from now on the same charge, or a bum trying to wrangle a night's sleep in a bus station. The other lawyers at the Defenders' table stopped talking; the pretty young attorney from the D.A.'s office put down her pen; the judge sat upright under the prepossessing robe. And there was a policeman standing behind Leland as there had not been for the others, someone watching to make sure this defendant stood in the position he was supposed to stand in, head facing straight ahead, hands clasped behind his back.

But even in that attentive silence, Nan could hardly hear. This is a show directed at one person, the judge, and unmindful of the spectators, however interested, sitting behind. "Dangerous weapon . . ." she made out. "Long record . . ." "Mother sitting in second row . . ." Would that rigid figure in the ladylike costume do any good? No, because the judge said, "Trial set for twelve-eighteen," and then he said, "Thirty thousand dollars bail," and it was over. The court officer was reading off a new number, and Leland, with the policeman still keeping him under surveillance, walked out the door for prisoners up front, and Gail, standing up, said, "Let's go," and Nan knew better than to ask whether there were sources to stake Leland to that thirty thousand.

But what about other times when money was not forthcoming? What about the years when even a third of thirty thousand might have helped? Nan all at once felt sick. She thought she might faint pushing through the dispirited hall, and standing outside, in air they kept telling you was warm for November, she had to lean against a wall.

"Didn't his father ever send money?" She couldn't bring herself to say the name.

"You mean his real father?"

Nan nodded. That's what she meant.

"I never asked him. I guess maybe he would have."

"Did he—know about him?"

"He surely knew when he was fourteen; I sent a newspaper clipping, even though it wasn't so bad, half a dozen of them involved that time, and the store was very nice about not bringing charges."

"Did he—the father—do anything then?"

Gail took off the hat. "What was to do? Ralph makes good money; that time he even hired our own lawyer. But four years later, by then he'd had it; he said let the Public Defenders take care of him, what they're there for."

"Did his father know that time?"

"He must have, the way it was splashed over all the papers, guns being involved and all."

Oh, William, how this must have torn you apart, you with your great pride, your expansive manner, your splendid stature designed to prefigure self-esteem.

Gail stepped back to let someone in a rush push out ahead—her time for rushing was over. "You always hear they're going to get training, something to work at when they get out, but they don't; all they do is meet those other punks."

"They might give him training this time."

"It's no use. He'll never be any good." Gail twisted the scarf as she spoke. "He was such a sweet baby. He talked at thirteen months, I taught him to say daddy first thing, I thought Ralph would be pleased. I don't know. Maybe if we hadn't had our own so fast, Ralph could have had time to get more attached to Leland. Or if he hadn't been such a puny kid."

Nan walked down the steps. "Funny, he should be so small, with William such a large man."

"William?" Gail said sharply. "Who said anything about William? Tad Collins was the father."

Chapter
ELEVEN

A NEW SURGE OF PEOPLE came out of the courthouse; she saw the family of the boy who'd been released without bail. Mother, father, sisters, brothers, making a victorious phalanx around him. "I don't understand."

"What's to understand?" Gail had no reason to hold herself together any longer. She stood with hat crumpled, head sunk on the double chin. "First Dr. Gardiner, then Dr. Collins. My loves. At least, dumb me, I thought they were my loves," she said, and for a second the voice was bitter enough to have issued from Miss Emory. "Caroline said the other day she might go in for nursing, but I told her over my dead body. Heaven forbid a daughter of mine. A smile from the great doctor and there you are, a pushover, your hair down and your legs wide open."

Another face from the courtroom, the man whose sleeping quarters were a chair in the bus station. "Well, not always," Nan murmured.

"You're right," Gail said. "I take it back. Actually, that one-two-three business, that's not how it was with Tad at all. You know how he got me? Kind of sweet, really. He talked about nurses. People who do the dirty work for doctors, only they never get to be doctors, not like lawyers, for instance, who do the grubbing and then move up; nurses stay nurses forever. Second-class citizens. Imagine me remembering that all these years. Talk like that, it was what we all used to chew over with each other, but I never heard anyone else pull it, surely not a doctor; who would suppose a doctor would have such ideas?"

"Who indeed," Nan said.

"He was a resident then. This cute-looking resident with blond hair and a smile that bowled you over. And he knew the subject cold. I mean, he wasn't just talking off the top of his head, he had a historical perspective."

She folded the scarf and put it in her bag: end of need for motherly dignity. "Did you know, for instance, that nurses used to have to stand up and give up their chairs when a doctor came into a room?"

Nan said as a matter of fact she did know.

"I can still hear it. One interesting fact like that after another. And no sex. That was the amazing thing. For the first couple of months he never even tried to hold my hand. Real respect. I mean, how can you not fall for a man like that."

"But sex later?" Nan said.

"God, yes. Sensational." Gail's laugh rang out over the sound of cars driving out of the parking lot. It was doing her good, this nostalgic detour to her days of erotic triumph. Color was back in her cheeks; under the flabby face, you could see the pretty girl who had won first one doctor and then another.

Nan opened her jacket; was the Washington air always so stifling? "And you're sure Dr. Collins was the father?"

Of course she was sure. Gail spoke with spirit.

"Maybe Dr. Gardiner himself didn't know. Maybe he thought—"

"How could he not know? He could see I was going with someone else. I hadn't been with him, except maybe to say hello in the hall, for five, no, it must've been six months when I found out I was pregnant."

She looked across at the gray building. At some lower

level, a place with wooden benches and locked doors, Leland would be waiting with the others for the bus to take him back to jail. "So it wasn't his mistake."

"Mistake?" Gail said.

"I mean, it's nothing he, well, thought about all these years?"

"He never thought about me so much at all. He was going with that other nurse by then. What was her name again? Marcy Drummond."

Nan stood still on the sidewalk, while the conflicting emotions buffeted her. On the one hand, inchoate relief: the squalid story doesn't pertain to William; her splendid husband had no connection to that boy with the surly mouth and dispirited gaze, his memory can remain inviolate. On the other hand, desolation. She is nowhere. She has to start over. This long morning in federal courthouse, and she has learned nothing.

Something must have shown in her face—Gail sounded remorseful. "I'm sorry. Here you are researching a book and I didn't tell you anything about Dr. Gardiner."

"You did, sort of."

"He was a sweet man, my first, like I said. But he was glad to shift to Marcy when I went with Tad. She was a stunner, that girl. I think it was Marcy he really cared for."

"Is it true that she too left the hospital under unhappy circumstances?"

"That Emory, she gave you an earful, didn't she? I'm not sure—breakdown, was what I heard. But breakdown, that can mean anything, can't it; in my experience all it means is people don't know what they're talking about. All I know is something went very wrong, so they had to let her go."

"Is she all right now?"

"All right?" Gail looked wearily at the courthouse, as if

to say, who could be all right, with all these inhuman forces rolling implacably over their lives. Then she said Marcy was never in good shape after that; she'd heard about some new trouble a couple of years ago, something ghastly but she couldn't be sure what. She wasn't really in touch; she just happened to run into someone from the hospital. Anyhow—Gail shook her head, as if clearing it of thoughts of Marcy; she had the self-centeredness of anyone whose own misery is overwhelming—anyhow, it was luck you needed. Say what you liked, however hard-working and decent you were, in the end what it came down to was plain dumb luck.

Well, maybe Gail was right. Look at her own luck, Nan thought when she finally drove away. She's seen all the people she tried to see, they all have been generous with their recollections, and what does it add up to? How does William shape up after all this talking? A talented young student whose family is willing to sacrifice his sister in the drive to push him ahead, an early dedication to research, a love life that includes passes at the pretty nurses, win some, lose some, a climb up the bureaucratic ladder—all the classic appurtenances to a shining medical career, so far they don't diverge in any appreciable way from the norm. Maybe they never will diverge in any appreciable way from the norm; she'll stay in her trap forever, Nan Dunlop Gardiner, believed by the world to have married a man for money and driven him to the despair of suicide.

Maybe she herself will believe it eventually. It can happen like that: the whole world convinced of your guilt, and their conviction so stirring, so infectious, that gradually you also accept it, you string along with that plausible collective view.

Maybe she was on the way to believing it now. As she steered her car through the frenetic traffic, she thought about William, and Tad, and William again. A man who was sixty-seven years old—did he really evoke in her an authentic passion? Wasn't it reasonable to suppose that in time she would have succumbed to Tad, that the canny propaganda and the chaste posture that were this man's efficacious trademarks would have led her, as they did Gail, to sensational sex, and that William, more percipient than she, had discerned that this would happen and thus had given up the fight?

No, it was not reasonable, it was nonsense, she would never fall for it. She pulled over to the side to study her street map—Marcy lived on a street called Maple in a place called Takoma Park. Marcy who left the hospital under dubious circumstances and then went downhill to more trouble—Marcy might be the one in a position to provide the answers.

Later she was to wonder at just what point she understood that Marcy would not be in a position to provide anything. When she walked up the half dozen steps to the porch of the two-family house on Maple and saw the green shades drawn all the way down? When she rang the bell and heard only silence? When, having gone back down the steps and then forced herself to return, she turned the doorknob and felt it give under her hand? No, it must have been when she stood in the hall, breathing in the physical smell of invalidism that after her years in a hospital any nurse knows so well.

Except in a hospital that essence is mingled with others: disinfectant, food, flowers, people, more disinfectant. Even in Aunt Martha's musty parlor, a window was opened from time to time; one was conscious of the wholesome scent from trees and grass outside the door. Here there was only that dour heaviness: quintessential invalidism pervading the hall.

She switched on a light. "Hello?" she said. "Hello!"
Nothing. But someone was inside, through the open door
on the left; she heard the rustle of sheets, the slurry growls
in a throat. She went to the door, then she stopped.

During her first week of nursing, she'd been sent around
at nine o'clock one night to a patient who had just been
admitted. "Well, hello there," she said to the woman lying
fully clothed on the bed. "We'll get you comfortable in a
jiffy," she said. "Are you hungry? Maybe I can rustle up
some fruit and crackers from the kitchen," she said. Then,
having met only the accusing gaze of those furious eyes on
the bed, she panicked and ran back to the desk. The panic
was of course inexcusable, but so, her supervisor nicely
told her, was her uninstructed assignment. "Aphasia," the
nurse said, "it's the most frustrating; they can't get anything out, not a word, not a syllable, and it drives them
wild, those unhappy stroke victims; it definitely should be
on the chart before a nurse is sent in."

So this was the ghastly thing Gail had heard. She stepped
closer to the woman on the bed; she picked up the right
hand that lay curved, pallid, clawlike, an emblem of disuse.
"Are you Marcy Drummond? Well, I'm a nurse," she said.
"Nan Dunlop. I work in New York, Gotham General Hospital, but I'm here in Washington for a while."

All at once, it was true. She was a nurse, not a detective;
the appurtenances of that alien profession slipped away;
nursing was in her hands, her voice, her expression, her
blood. She was a nurse and she had taken care of plenty of
stroke victims since that misguided entry into an unlabeled
room, and as her hands began their practiced movements
she saw she was having a nurse's beneficent effect; the tense
knees relented under the rumpled sheets, the left hand
stopped its frenzied plucking at the blanket, the glaring
eyes shifted from hostility to a guarded calm.

"Mind if I fix your bed?" she asked, and the woman moved her lips. "No," she got out, "No."

"Well, you can talk a little, can't you? Can you also say yes?"

A hoarse yes emerged from the straining throat.

"Well, good. Yes and no. Can you say anything else?" But the fierceness came back into her eyes, as if all the helplessness of her body were focused in those dark pupils, and Nan spoke quickly, her hands keeping up their accustomed rites. "Yes and no, they're most important, aren't they, as long as you have them—now, if I give you a push, think you can get to the other side of the bed so I can work on this side?"

There was plenty of work. Not just smoothing out sheets and straightening blankets, but easing apprehension. Any unexpected motion startled her, so the fright came back into her eyes; her good hand clutched at whatever was near. Aren't you used to being taken care of, Nan wanted to ask, knew enough not to ask. Besides, the paraphernalia of care was all around; someone at some time must put this paralyzed creature into the wheelchair over by the window, feed her from the tray, arrange the glass and straw where her serviceable left hand can reach them, get her into the slippers and bathrobe stationed alongside the bed.

"Goodness, your hands are sticky. Guess they didn't wash you off after lunch; mind if I wet this rag and—There! That feels better, doesn't it?"

"Yes."

No, yes, no, yes. Her repertoire. A repertoire she obviously takes satisfaction in using, so when Nan says, "The bed looks better now," she says Yes, yes, yes, yes, a woman giving her all.

"Now maybe I can comb your hair if you'll try to sit up."
Trying to sit her up involved sliding a hand behind her

back, pushing on the right, the damaged, side, while Marcy tugged in what seemed a contradictory motion, but eventually the process got her upright enough so Nan could get the comb from the dresser and start combing. Then she stopped combing.

Dear God, Gail was right. A stunner. Or, rather, she once was a stunner. Or, rather, now that she's sitting up, you can see the relics of beauty that once must have made her a stunner: the wonderful bone structure, wide mouth, deep eyes, tawny coloring. At a time when, if you can further believe Gail, William had really cared for her, this woman with the angry eyes and lifeless skin must have been one of the beauties.

Nan stood holding the comb. Once last winter when one of her patients had been hospitalized after stroke, the woman's daughter had stopped her outside the door. "She used to be so elegant, Christ, isn't it awful? If it was me I'd rather be dead." Marcy, would you rather be dead than stuck here, a ruin, unable to talk, powerless to move, in a cotton nightgown? Nan was tugging at the gown, pulling it down over the flabby breasts, when she heard someone at the door.

"What do you think you're doing here?" A sensible question, directed to her, the interloper. Nan turned, she saw a woman in a gray suit standing in the doorway.

"I'm a nurse. Nan Dunlop. I fixed her bed a little, I thought I'd just—"

"How'd you get in?" The same wide mouth, high cheekbones, green-flecked eyes as Marcy, but without the element that made for beauty. This woman, in fact, was so stolid, so commonplace looking, as to be almost plain.

"Oh, well, the door was open, so when no one answered . . ."

"Who gave you the right to come in?"

"Well, I did ring a couple of times."

"What do you think you're doing here?"

Back to the basic question, and with it, Nan saw, her original role. Standing next to the bed in this steamy room, she was not a nurse, no, not remotely entitled to march under that salutary title. Here in a house where she didn't belong, she was a detective, someone primed for the most offensive of duties, which was to ferret out facts others would just as soon keep hidden and to elicit emotions, mainly defensiveness and anger, people would just as soon not experience.

The anger was now turned elsewhere. "Marcy, you bad girl, you didn't finish your lunch."

From the bad girl, a guttural mumble.

"Mrs. Moss left the tray in the kitchen; I can see you left half the meat loaf. I just don't understand it. You know what I go through to get you decent food, and you won't even make the little effort to eat it." She turned to Nan. "It does aggravate you. There I am trying to keep a little order in a classroom all day, and on the way home do I take the easiest route? No, I go five minutes out of my way to this butcher, and then another five, just about, till I find a place to park, all because the stuff is better than you get in the supermarket; I think maybe she'll enjoy it. But then when she takes for granted, she won't even cooperate. . . ."

She, she, she—as if Marcy were a child incapable of understanding. Well, in the mind of a sister, Marcy is a child incapable of understanding. The old syndrome: Nan is used to it. What a good girl to do all her exercises, the family will say to the white-haired woman lying limp on the bed. You be a good boy now, they murmur in farewell to the stricken grandfather. Inevitable. They can be told again and again that intelligence is unimpaired, the brain functions are intact, but they don't believe it; they can't—

anyone who can't articulate his thoughts must be un-
qualified for thinking. Indeed, she sometimes falls into the
error herself. Don't cry, there's a good girl, she will say in
helpless comfort.

Marcy was crying now, those facile tears which along
with uninhibited laughter are a symptom of the stroke
victim. Tears ran down the pasty cheeks, so her sister went
up to her. "Stop crying; I'm not angry, not a bit. You cold?
You want to pee? Okay, you be a good girl now and get
some rest while I clean up inside."

Marcy did rest; at least her hand stopped plucking at the
sheet, and she closed her eyes, and the other two escaped
into the kitchen, where the tray with the unappreciated
meat loaf was on the table. Big Sister Is Watching You.

"It really is hard," the woman said. "You want to do the
best for her, keep up her health, but when she won't even
eat her lunch after all that trouble. Of course if I'd give her
cake or ice cream she'd gobble that up quick enough. But
she's not allowed—she's diabetic; the Visiting Nurses told
me no sweets at all. Sometimes I give her a little plain
Jell-O, but even that you're taking a chance." Linda put
grocery bags up on the table and began unpacking. Canned
soup, oranges, dry cereal, a cake box. She saw Nan's eyes
on the box. "Oh, I won't let her see. I'm careful not to bring
her in the kitchen; when I have her in the wheelchair we
go the other way so she won't feel bad. But I have to have
a life too, don't I?"

"Oh, yes," Nan said quickly.

"Look, my name is Linda Drummond. I'm her sister."

"Nan Dunlop. Glad to meet you." Peace. Talking quietly
to each other in the small kitchen, they were—not friends,
no reason for that; rather, accomplices. There was a bond.
By virtue of not being sick, they were a couple, a club;
theirs was the capacity for exclusion. You saw it happen all

the time; even though, a conscientious nurse, you guarded against it, you saw it happen. How is he *really*, the visitor would whisper, standing at the door or walking up and down the hall. Even in the sickroom it could happen: a meaningful look across a bed, a lift of eyebrows, and that silent dialogue was established; you were in involuntary cahoots. The well against the ailing. Two against one.

Linda took more cans out of the bags and asked if Nan had been sent by the Visiting Nurses.

"Me? Oh, no. Actually, I'm here doing research on a doctor. William Gardiner—does the name ring a bell? He's someone I think your sister knew a long time ago. When I decided to come by I had no idea she was sick."

The face that lacked a sister's beauty looked only partly mollified. "You here for the day?"

"The day? Heavens, no. I'm here for weeks. Months," she said firmly. True. If I have to, I'll stay and stay, she had told Tad, and she was just beginning to realize how necessary it might be.

"Do you have a decent hotel? Once in a great while a friend comes to visit, and I can't ask them to sleep here, God knows, and if I knew some nice clean place, not too expensive."

Nan told her the name.

"Clean, you say? Quiet? I'll remember." Linda was at the window; the eyes that were like Marcy's and not like them were taking everything in. "And you rented a car?"

"No, the car is mine. I drove down from New York." Inquisition finished? Had she established her credentials? Evidently, because Linda resumed unpacking the groceries. Nan watched a minute, then she said she was glad at least Linda had a woman to help with the nursing.

"Fat lot of help. She comes at ten, leaves at two. She's supposed to bathe her, clean the room, make the lunch, but half the time when I get back there's all the work to do myself."

Nan looked at the wall clock. Ten past four. "And she's always alone like this, from two until now?"

"Listen, I'm lucky to have a job teaching. If I worked in an office, a regular desk job, I wouldn't be home till six; she'd have to be by herself even longer." Linda spoke with mechanical indignation: Was this something she kept telling Marcy? Stop crying now, you should be grateful I'm here at all, you bad girl.

"Then the whole responsibility is on you?"

"There is no one else. Our parents are dead. We have a brother in L.A. but he has three kids; it's all he can do to support them."

"Terrible," Nan murmured. "A stroke. The worst, just about."

"Terrible. Yes." She means for herself, Nan saw. Well, she's entitled. They suffer a servitude too, these reluctant custodians.

"Sometimes I get so fed up I could scream," Linda said.

"Oh, I know."

"But you can't scream at her. Poor thing, it's not her fault and I just want to help her, you know what I mean?"

Very well. Linda meant in a way it *was* Marcy's fault— how often, from distressed relatives, has she seen that ambivalence? They are very caring, all those troubled spouses and children and siblings and friends. Doctor, should we try to get a second opinion? Isn't there some other drug? What if we get an extra nurse? And their own efforts are unremitting. They bring ingenious treats; they sit for hours in smiling sympathy; they devise tactful methods of communication; they plan elaborate rearrangements of their homes to accommodate the paraphernalia of illness.

At the same time, they dream of their own liberation; the

sense of it is always with them. You really think, Doctor,
it might be pneumonia—and you can hear the involuntary
exultation: hope masquerading as decent anxiety. Dear
lord, to be free, if pneumonia would indeed take hold,
overcome that grotesque body that otherwise is going to
hold us tied to it forever.

And now, here was Linda, a member of the club. She was
devoted; oh, she truly was, her life an assertion of love and
dedication. Look how she rushed home after school, day
after day that relentless schedule, and paid the attendant
out of her meager earnings, and then the shopping, a real
butcher—it would be easier at the supermarket, but no, the
poor thing has so little pleasure, let's give her the best meat.
And it was all true, absolutely, a life devoted to keeping
Marcy going.

At the same time, she can't bear it. When you think about
it, you realize she really cannot bear it. The poor thing, she
says, and you feel the revulsion. Can't I have a life of my
own? she says, and unrolled is the panorama of her unwill-
ing sacrifice. Want to pee? she says to a forty-five-year-old
sister, and you hear the need to humiliate, remind the patient that for all purposes she's a child.

Nan pushed back her chair and asked how long ago
Marcy had had the stroke.

"Three years now. She was forty-two."

"Odd. At that age they usually make more of a recovery."

Linda was working faster. Apples, eggs, margarine, milk,
each item set down in emphatic counterpoint to her words.
"Oh, sure. They recover if they're willing to do the things
that help them recover. There's all that special equipment,
marvelous new techniques—right at the start I made a
study. A whole wing in the hospital for physical therapy,
speech therapy—the works. When I was looking around,
there was a girl, just about the same age as Marcy, and after

six months she was talking so you could understand, and walking with a cane—she could even dress herself. Well, being a nurse, you know all about it. But someone, like I said, has to be willing."

"You mean, she wouldn't do the exercises?"

"I mean, she wouldn't set foot in a hospital." Bread crumbs, set down with a vicious little thump. "She got hysterical if we even tried to get her out of the car."

"But why?"

"Oh, why." Still that tone of languid irritableness. "How can you find out anything from someone who can't talk? If you knew what questions to ask, she could give you a yes or no answer. But if you knew what questions to ask, you wouldn't have to ask them." Thump, thump for the scouring powder, the soap.

Nan watched those assiduous hands. "Another odd thing is her getting a stroke at all. At her age, one usually doesn't."

"She was in bad shape. Even in those days, she wouldn't see a doctor."

"Bad shape how?"

"She had a nervous breakdown. That was twenty, oh, maybe twenty-one years ago. Nothing was ever right for her after that."

Nan opened her mouth, closed it, said finally nervous breakdown was just a phrase. Catch-all. It meant nothing.

Linda opened a cabinet and started putting away the groceries.

"Nervous breakdown—is that what they said when she had to leave the hospital?" Nan persisted.

"Don't ask me what anyone said. I was a kid. I was still at school myself," Linda said with emphatic point. "No one told me anything, but I heard rumors."

"Rumors like what?"

"She went nuts, my sister did. She'd been this cracker-jack nurse; she must have been because she just got a raise, and then all of a sudden she couldn't keep records straight. She forgot which patient was which. She made mistakes about medications." Linda folded the paper bags; more methodical thumping. "She was a beautiful thing, and she went off her rocker," Linda said in a flat voice, as if the two were related.

But they were not related, even though a plain-faced sister would like to think so. After all, look at me—suddenly she remembered William: You remind me of someone. . . . Oh, Marcy, you were like me twenty years ago, I just know it. The same pretty face under the pert white cap, the same mixture of warm friendliness and snappy competence. You were the one—so easy to picture—with time for that five-minute talk with the patient going down for an operation. You knew the tone of casual disdain to use to the man who made passes when you bathed him. You listened to the feats of superhuman contrivance that enabled the woman with six children to sit all day beside her dying husband. And you were in love, so when you doled out the medication, your hand was a little more steady, your concentration more intense, because of the image of that splendid doctor who was taking you out that night to dinner and dancing. So why did you fall into that ambiguous hole they call a nervous breakdown, why?

"I heard that a couple of patients almost died because she forgot to give them injections. Well, naturally they had to let her go, you can't take chances with a nurse who—"

Who what? There were whimpering noises from the room across the hall, guttural cries that got louder, shriller. "She can't stand it if she thinks you're talking about her," Linda said as they hurried in. "Marcy dear, I was just telling Miss Dunlop I'm going to fix you a nice cheese omelet for supper."

Marcy dear beat furiously with her good hand against the sheet.

"You hungry, dear? Should I fix your pillow? Sure you don't want to pee?"

"Maybe she didn't like what you were saying about the hospital. About why they had to let her go," Nan said and watched a ray of gratification break over that ruined face.

"Okay, I won't say it, I take it back. Listen, dear, I'm going to bring you a nice glass of juice—not frozen, I bought fresh oranges—so you wait here like a good girl. Miss Dunlop is just going; I'll see her out."

Well, Miss Dunlop might as well go; there was little information to be found in this fetid room. Linda had it right: if you knew what questions to ask, you wouldn't have to ask them.

Chapter
TWELVE

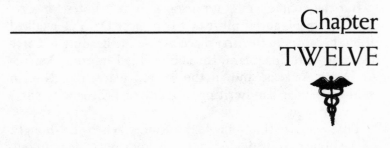

BACK, THEN, TO THE MOTEL, to the room that had been accurately described as being clean, neat, quiet, not too expensive. Back feeling more burdened, really, because having started the day thinking the world held only the one problem of why a man like William commits suicide, she now found herself enmeshed in the different one of why a nurse with everything going for her falls apart.

She would feel better after she took a shower. It was what she did every day when she came home from work, that spirited washing that almost, though never quite, expunged the hospital. And it was true, by the time she went down to dinner, she no longer heard the shrill little whimpers; she had pushed back the image of a woman with her beauty gone to parchment skin and agitated eyes. Dinner was good clam chowder and indifferent trout to go with the nautical decorations, and afterwards—back to business— she took out the notes she had found in the evaluation folder. She took them without any real hope: another layer to add to the pile of records and memos and outlines and laconic reports already pored over. But anything William wrote called for attention, and she settled herself in a corner of the couch. Then she stood; she went to the desk, where the light, though still inadequate, was better. Steady, now. Just because you catch a few insistent words, don't jump, read carefully, avoid the quick conclusion.

But the conclusion is unmistakable: it is notes for a research project, and it must be the project Dr. Tyler talked about because, in the first place, while the heading is Early Dose of Anti-Coagulant, the subhead is Limiting Damage in Heart Attacks, and in the second place, the date, in William's clear handwriting, is a day in February twenty-one years ago.

That handwriting—she had to smile. When she thought of the notations by doctors she had laboriously deciphered, those crabbed, irate scrawls that say I'm somebody, I put in my time getting where I am, now you can struggle a little too. William's handwriting, on the other hand, was like him: large confident letters that jolly you, draw you on. She even understood the context, and why not—didn't she know he was a born teacher? Her eye skimmed the page, and it was as if she were standing behind the medical students in the hospital amphitheater, while his resonant voice went on making everything lucid, simple, reasonable. Oh, William!

Concept

I propose to institute an early treatment of a high but safe dose of anti-coagulant to individuals who suffer an unexpected heart attack caused by a potentially lethal rhythm of the heart beat. The purpose is to prevent a clot from developing in one or more of the major coronary arteries.

It is well known that the formation of such clots is the most important cause of damage to the heart muscles, resulting in either death or severe impairment. Since recent progress has made it possible for well-equipped resuscitation teams to get to a large number of patients and temporarily restore the heart to normal rhythm, the early dose of anti-coagulant may prevent the clot from forming and leave these patients with a better prognosis for future recovery.

Design

To test the hypothesis, one hundred patients will be needed as the treatment group, and the same number matched as to age and other conditions for the control group. Of course the control group will be treated with all appropriate methods used presently, but they will not receive the experimental anti-coagulant.

Note: Consult a statistician in the field of cardiac research to help set up a research design with the proper relative proportion of treated patients to untreated. (Mrs. Josephine Springer has expressed considerable interest. Together with her husband Bert—old money—she may be willing to provide financial backing.)

Results

March 8. In the first two months, 8 patients tested. The 4 who were treated with anti-coagulants consisted of a 55-year-old man suffering his second coronary, a 43-year-old woman, a 60-year-old man also suffering from emphysema, and a 40-year-old man who happens to be an assistant secretary of state. The 4 controls consisted of a 52-year-old man, a 45-year-old woman, a 55-year-old man with severe arthritic problems, and a 44-year-old man with a demanding professional life. Of the 4 treated cases, all except the 60-year-old man recovered without any development of coronary clots and did not develop myocardial infarction. The 60-year-old man died of a myocardial infarction five days after entering the hospital. Of the 4 controls, 3 developed coronary clots—1 died and 2 had severe damage to the heart muscle. One, the woman, did not develop a clot. This is a favorable beginning, but far from conclusive.

April 10.

That was it. The month heralded, the record stopped. Well, why does a man stop a project when it's just getting under way? A couple of obvious reasons. Someone being treated develops an adverse reaction, or he decides the whole idea is a bad one. But had the anti-coagulant adversely affected one of those four treated patients, William would have been the first to say so, and as for the whole concept being faulty, he'd decided just the opposite, which was favorable.

Favorable: a word, in his restrained, temperate idiom, whose equivalent was Hooray, keep it up, bingo, great. Well, why would William renounce a project he thought was great? Personal reasons, he had told his good friend Dr. Tyler, but he had never allowed personal reasons, whatever that meant, to disrupt his professional life; he surely would not condone their impinging on a project that might be destined to save lives. She sat holding the papers, and for some reason Victor's voice slid into her mind. "There are depths. Rare and complicated aspects." Well, of course. I loved the idea of those complicated aspects; I was ready to devote my whole being to respecting them, indulging them, accommodating to them. But I didn't know, no one told me, I would have to embark on a search to reconstruct them—for a second she felt anger flooding her. Anger at whom? For what? She sat another minute, then she laid the papers with the others and went to the phone; when she came back, she had an appointment at ten-thirty the next morning with a Mrs. Josephine Springer who lived on Foxhall Road.

Foxhall Road could be reached, according to her road map, through a maze of diagonal avenues, which, like all Washington diagonal avenues, would not reveal their true nature till one was driving on them. Should she take a taxi, leave to someone equipped to deal with them the imponderables of Washington traffic? No, she had done all right so far, relying on nerve and street maps, and it was better to have one's own car so an exit could be made at the moment and in the manner of one's choosing. Also, if her hunch was correct, Foxhall Road denoted affluence, and for this, William's imperial green car should strike the appropriate note.

Her own car, then, and a tweed suit, and her suede shoes, she thought next morning—high style to meet old money. And decent weather at last. The humidity had lifted; it was the kind of day that in New York impelled from her the tribute of a brisk step and involuntary smile. Also, as she walked up the incline of the parking lot she saw in the glance of a man coming in the other direction the grin that told her the suit was a success: Lady, you look *good*.

Well, she'd better look good. Her fifth interview—God, no, sixth—in which she must assume an alien persona in order to disarm an unknowable stranger, and for a second she yearned for someone she knew, someone old shoe, whose reactions were calculable in advance. Tad, for instance; if she could just talk to him on the phone, hear the familiar voice and project onto it the pleasant face slipping into its predictable smile. Even Victor, whose vitriolic look was at least a known quantity, an anchor, something, in this new city, to be counted on.

No, what was the matter with her, of course not Victor. Never Victor, she thought as she got into the car. She would, in fact, like never to see Victor again; Victor who distrusted her, despised her, would be gratified by the peculiar way the car was acting. Acting for what reason? What vital step did she omit? She did what she always does: key in, emergency brake off, hands on that solid steering wheel, finger on brake—why was she sliding at unconscionable speed toward the concrete wall straight ahead instead of gliding slowly so she could make the turn halfway down, and drive past the small wooden shelter where no attendant ever sits, and with the road map spread out on her lap, turn left onto the street? She tried to turn, a ferocious tug on the wheel coupled with a frantic pull on the brakes. But she was going faster, she was up against the wall, and the crashing noise signified damage to William's car and ruin to the spindly bushes growing in an insufficient bed at the foot of the wall, and might also, she understood as pain bit her, denote irremediable harm to herself.

She opened her eyes to meet the gaze of strangers. Their intent look must be because she is in reality two people. She is the assortment of limbs and appendages hunched over the wheel, with blood trickling down her wrist and a startling numbness gripping her whole middle section; she is also the detached observer who from her vantage point of cynical experience is able to judge the performance of those who participate. C minus, then, for the hasty, the really crude way in which they pull her from the car, so if a broken neck is among her injuries she will be paralyzed for life. B for the self-important brusqueness with which they hold back those who arrive later and want to see everything, and another B for the speed with which the ambulance comes. B plus, make it A minus, she thinks drowsily, for whatever medication the tall white-garbed medic inserts into her arm, and A for the dexterity—no chances about broken necks this time—with which they lift her onto a stretcher and then through the ambulance's hospitably open door. And A for the delicacy of that same lanky medic who says Shh, she can hear everything, when his colleagues start on a ghoulish speculation about her fate. Actually, she couldn't hear. She was conscious of moving at great speed—someone else having to tussle with Washington traffic after all—but she knew nothing of the end of her journey or her entry into the emergency room. Must be an emergency room, she thought when she opened her eyes, all the familiar trappings: the policeman standing stolid beside the desk, and the nurse coming in and then, distractedly, rushing out, and the intern who said, Be a minute now, and the inadequate curtain that separated her from the man in the next alcove, so she could hear him yelling, Millie, someone get Millie, and when someone pushed aside the curtain she could also see the bloodied bandage around his head.

Well, she wished for it, didn't she? Something old shoe: God knows an emergency room was that. It was like the fairy tale, where the woman gets her wishes, but in so distorted, so cruelly perverse a fashion that her last wish must be for everything to be back as it was. I take it back, she wanted to say. I changed my mind. But she was stuck, the implacable process was going on during which nothing one says can make a difference; when the intern said, We'll have you all right in no time, she didn't argue; she forbore to point out that she was a nurse and as such capable of absorbing more informative statements; she simply closed her eyes and lay quiet for the trip upstairs.

Upstairs she continued quiet. From time to time she and Rosanne used to speculate about what it was like to be a patient. How do they really feel, those creatures subject to the whims of distracted authority? Well, now she knew. She must know because she was caught up in the standard patient syndrome. She was conscious of her pain increasing in direct proportion to the time it took for someone to answer her bell. She automatically loathed the woman with dyed hair and bloated face who shared her room. She asked petulantly why they had to wake her up to give her sleeping medicine. And when a doctor came in to tell her they were encouraged—no damage, after all, to the spleen, and also it didn't look like a skull fracture, but still there was a dark spot on the X-rays, they would just keep her quiet another day to make sure—when this cursory report was given, she didn't ask for specifics; she simply folded her arms and regarded him with the docility of one grateful for even this limited attention.

But he didn't walk out, this doctor. He lifted her hand on which he'd already felt the pulse, looked again at her chart, had a word with the nurse, and cleared his throat. Was he right in thinking she was in no great discomfort at the moment? Well, yes, that superficial cut on the wrist, and of course her head, they didn't want her moving more than was necessary, but if it wouldn't bother her too much, there was someone who'd like to talk to her.

"Someone?" She was conscious of the woman in the other bed lying with alert breath.

"The police would like to ask you some questions about the accident."

She breathed deeply. She'd blotted it all out. The wall, the speed, the crowds, the broken bush uprooted from its meager bed—the only way to bear such images was to blot them out. "What time is it?" Her first request for information.

"Nine thirty."

"Nine thirty at night?" But a glance out the window

showed the truth; a day had gone by since that demonstration of inept driving on her part. "I don't even know what hospital this is."

He told her and waited.

Not William and Tad's hospital; she couldn't pull rank even if she wished to. She hoisted herself up on the pillow. What she wanted to say was could she have a mirror. Instead she said sure, let them come in.

Them was one, a policeman with sharp features and a look of such unease that she glanced down at herself. Sheet slipped sideways? Stretch of naked thigh exposed? Breast emerging from open neck of hospital gown?

There was less unease when he began to talk. He said she was lucky. If her car had made it out to the street, or if she'd been parked father from the wall with consequently more time to work up speed, or even if her car had been less solid, with any of those contingencies, she could be in lots worse shape than she is now. A close call, that is to say. In the police department, they don't like close calls; they believe it's in everyone's interest to prevent them.

She moved higher on the pillow. "You mean, I should have had the car checked. Every month, I know, but I'm not really accustomed . . ."

But he shook his head. A car check was not what he had in mind. In fact, the brake line was cut.

"Brake line?" She was ignorant of mechanics; she'd always found it convenient to be ignorant of mechanics. She had friends who changed tires, tested oil, looked knowledgeably under hoods, but she had never felt the desire to add this expertise to her fields of competence. She could appreciate, however, that a brake line should not be cut.

"You know what happens," he said as if she did. "Fluid drains out; we did in fact find some where you had been parked."

"Fluid," she repeated.

"When you pushed on the brake pedal, instead of that compressing the fluid which then pushes the brake shoes against the wheels, the fluid went squirting out."

She understood isolated words—wheels, pedal, shoes— but she couldn't form them into an image, still less relate them to what had happened. "Then a check-up . . ." she hopefully said.

"Mrs. Gardiner, I don't think you understand. There was no brake fluid because someone tampered with the brake line."

"Ah." Impossible to misunderstand further, if only because the others in the room—a nurse and the woman in the next bed—were tingling with excited understanding. Cutting a line, is that hard to do? she absurdly asked.

But he treated it like a reasonable question and said it was just a matter of lying under the car, taking out the wire-cutting pliers, locating the line, which was made of some soft metal—he forgot if hers was copper or tin—and snip, snip.

"But couldn't that happen by accident?"

It could, but in all probability it didn't. Her line had been cleanly, unmistakably cut. Which is why he wonders what she's doing in Washington.

Silence, while she absorbed this non sequitur. A woman with pail and mop came in, and the nurse told her to clean in another room first, and with an angry clatter—someone always making it hard for you—the woman went out. "My husband just died," Nan said inanely.

"Yes, I know."

She lay motionless. Of course he knew everything; how could she suppose not? They look into pocketbooks for identification and under car hoods for sabotage, and they also have instantly available to them every specific about one's past: "Young Widow Inherits Money." Smash a car into the wall of an obscure parking lot, and the computers of two cities go into action.

And now he was waiting to know more: who might have wanted her to smash into that wall? She moved the sheet decorously up to her chin and said she was interviewing people in connection with the circumstances of her husband's death.

"Could you be more precise, Mrs. Gardiner?"

Be precise while lying flat with authority looming above one? "My husband committed suicide." She spoke with careful pedantry, as if he weren't up on the whole story. "I mean, he left a note, and I don't think it means what it was thought to mean, so I'm talking to people who knew him long ago."

"That's why you came, to talk to people who knew him long ago?"

Another rebuff from the vigilant nurse: an attendant with the juice cart told to try later. She said yes, that's why she came.

"Have you been successful in finding people to interview?"

She said yes, definitely; she'd talked to five people who had known her husband well.

He made a little mark in his notebook—is he really writing down the number 5? "These friends of your late husband, did any of them show resentment at your questions?"

"Just the opposite. They all were glad to talk; they remembered him well; they were delighted to share their memories." She heard her tone. Fatuous. Effusive. Like someone reporting on a picnic, a class party. "Actually, there is someone here who resents me."

"What's her name?"

She saw the woman on the next bed easing forward on

her elbow. "A he. Victor Hemmings. He was my husband's lawyer, but he's in Washington now; I think he's staying at the Hilton. But that's crazy," she added quickly. "Just because he mistrusts me, he thinks I —well, whatever he thinks he would never want to harm me. Not physically, I mean. Besides, he's probably not even here anymore; I just happened to run into him for a second."

"Hemmings. How do you spell it?"

Oh, God, he was writing it down—something else for the computers to tear into. They'd look him up and interrogate him—it could only make him hate her more. "Listen, I didn't mean . . ."

But the policeman was studying his notes, as if to issue some statement that would grandly sum them up. What he said, however, was that he was a little surprised to hear that she was doing some investigating on her own because it was his impression that the New York police were the ones carrying on an investigation.

"Investigation of what?"

"As you mentioned, the circumstances of your husband's death," he said with heavy courtesy. "I believe they said there was some question about sleeping pills."

"A question?"

"About your having been the one to supply them."

Surely one should be upright at such a moment, head high, voice resonant to conceal the pounding heart. "Oh, no, that's all wrong, you must have misunderstood; that was cleared up, the police were perfectly—"

Perfectly what? She heard Victor's voice: Do you really think the police are satisfied? She was conscious that the room had changed again. The woman in the next bed had swung herself around for better viewing, the nurse was standing with hand arrested over the tray for medication. Just like that moment when Leland stood up in the courtroom. I'm like Leland, she thought. Someone in a category that merits watching. Thinking of my possible past actions, people stiffen into attentive silence.

She spoke with great resolution. Since the police thought someone had tampered—was that his word?—with her car, she now wondered what they were going to do about it.

"Based on the information you've given us, Mrs. Gardiner, I don't know that at this point there's anything we can do. We'll have to consult with the New York authorities, of course."

"But I'm here in Washington."

He said with scrupulous ambiguity that of course the two cases were related.

"You mean, if the New York police don't think I'm worthy of protection, you won't be inclined to give it to me?"

But she had gone too far. Stated things too baldly. He said it was hard to see in what exact way they could exactly help her. But they were surely available; she must get in touch with them in case the situation in any way changed. Meanwhile, he expressed hopes for her prompt recovery, and reminded her to notify her insurance agent when she felt stronger. Then he left, and the nurse went after him.

A burst of activity followed their exit. A nurse came in with a pitcher of juice, and after her another nurse to take temperatures, and then another to tell the roommate to take this pill, just swallow it down, dear, and then someone with clean linen that she left on a chair, and someone else . . . Well, maybe they were all watching out for her; that explained the dizzying attention. Or maybe exactly the opposite—the policeman said crazy dame in there, some hanky panky with her husband, and we want to know what's going on, so keep an eye.

"Don't you worry. I'm right here taking care of you." The woman in the next bed.

"You are?"

"Every second. You go to sleep whenever you feel like; no one's going to get at you while Jessica Fay is watching out."

My protector. Mrs. Fay has a tube going in one nostril and a catheter snaking out from under the bed, and the wound from what must be a recent operation gapes like an opening in the earth when the nurse comes to clean it, but she's going to protect me. Ludicrous. Ludicrous but sweet. Why did I think I didn't like her, this woman looking at me tenderly from under the dyed, disheveled hair?

In fact she didn't want to sleep; she was getting stronger every minute, and she wanted to think about all the details that a hospital stay would have made it necessary to attend to. The insurance agent, obviously, and she ought to get word to the motel that she'd be back, and she must apologize to that moneyed Mrs. Springer for the broken appointment and also attempt to make another, and she'd better see about her clothes—she knew what could happen to one's belongings in an emergency admission, so as soon as she had her energy she'd make sure her nice suit and good suede shoes were all right—and as for her medical condition, she must find out which doctor was in charge and elicit from him an accurate description of her injuries. Anything else? It could wait. She'd take a little rest after all. Rest and dismiss everything. But when she closed her eyes, Linda appeared. A Linda grotesquely bent over because she's carrying Marcy on her back. What hotel are you staying at? Linda asks from her distorted position. Is that your car? Linda says, as she shifts under the cumbersome weight. Eat this meat loaf, Linda says, I'm going to stand right here and watch till you eat it so stop crying; crying won't do you any good.

"Take it easy, honey, don't cry." Her roommate was leaning toward her.

She pulled herself upright.

"You're going to be all right; look, they don't even have you on IV."

"Oh, I know."

"You heard that policeman. By some miracle, not hurt, he wouldn't say it if they hadn't told him. I bet when Dr. Allen comes in he'll discharge you."

She said it wasn't exactly her physical condition.

"You mean all that about the police in New York?" The woman smiled kindly at her. "Honey, don't let it throw you. That's their dumb mentality, blowing everything up so it sounds much worse than it really is."

She smiled back, because how could she explain that what threw her was the mentality that enabled them to consider one person simultaneously as victim and as suspect.

Chapter
THIRTEEN

DR. ALLEN DID DISCHARGE HER that afternoon. Standing at the foot of her bed, he said all the tests were negative: no signs of fracture or internal bleeding. That wrist, of course, a nasty cut; he'll give her a prescription for an ointment she should put on when she changes the bandage once a day, but it should heal within a week. Any headaches, she should call his office right away, but he anticipates no trouble. And she should of course be careful.

Careful? She looked up. Careful of the person who tampered with the brake fluid of her car? But if he had heard of this problematic effort, he didn't say so; what he meant, plainly, was that she should not overstrain herself. Eat regularly. Get a good night's sleep. Stop when she gets tired. Sensible precautions—he gave them in his bored voice—for one whose nervous system has had a shock. Oh, and she should drive a car again within the next couple of days. The old theory: get back on the horse. In his experience, sound advice. Now. Does she have any questions?

Yes. If he knew who she was, rather who her husband had been, would he be less perfunctory? Give different warnings? Advise more stringent measures?

But in fact she didn't need more stringent measures. If as a nurse she knew anything, it was how to assess the workings of her own body, and that dependable mechanism went creditably about its business; look at the dinner she tucked away in the nautical resturant that evening, or the way she slept through the night, eight hours straight, or even the sprightly step with which next morning she went on an experimental walk around the block. It was true that her heart beat faster when she passed the parking lot. There it was, the broken wall, the shattered bricks, the crassly uprooted bushes. Someone had shoveled bricks and dirt in a pile, but otherwise everything remained as it was when they carried her off. Scene of the crime: You were supposed to return to it for clues, but though she walked up to her old parking place and down again to the unattended debris, it told her nothing. Well, maybe there was nothing to tell, and by the time she went back to the lobby and called a taxi for that reconstituted appointment with the Springers, her pulse was again normal, her breathing under control.

The Springers' was a good house to come to in a taxi; with someone else doing the driving, one was free to get a full sense of spacious vistas and noble proportions. One also got the sense of casual neglect. How different from that showplace of William's sister, where everything was rigorously calculated to say polish, style, newness, chic. Old money doesn't have to put on a show; the leaves can lie unraked in a great rust carpet under the beech trees, weeds can grow luxuriously between the flagstones on the walk, paint peels in abundant tendrils on the front columns. And when the maid led the way through half a dozen paneled rooms, her gaze rested with jaunty composure on the dusty mantels and dilapidated chairs.

Mrs. Springer was sitting in a small, bright sunroom. "My dear, how d'you do? I'm Josephine Springer; my husband Bert will be down in a few minutes. If he knew how pretty you were, he'd be down right now. Well, why am I surprised? He had an eye, your husband did; I wouldn't have expected him to marry a frump, not William. You don't mind if I call him William, do you? It's what he insisted on as soon as we got to know each other. None of that fake dignity most doctors think they have to go in for. The Great Herr Doctor—not for him. Bert, this is Mrs. Gardiner, you remember I told you, she wants to ask us questions for a book about dear William. Mrs. Gardiner, my husband Bert."

They looked alike. At least they had the same wavy white hair, the same energetic eyes under bushy white eyebrows, the same tanned, wrinkled skin stretched across small, round faces.

"Bert, I've been telling her about William. Remember how he'd come in, like a big rush of wind, and squeeze you in one of his great hugs, that darling man, and sit right in that chair you're in now? Torn, I see; one of these days we have to get it fixed. Well, your William. What a man he was. Beautiful and bright—Bert, didn't I say so?"

"You surely did, all the time."

"So did you."

"Well, not quite the same way, my sweet; I didn't dream about going to bed with him."

"Bert, you know I didn't. I mean, I didn't go."

"He didn't ask you, did he?"

"Bert, we shouldn't talk like this, her husband after all."

Nan sat demurely. Only the very rich, she thought. They can let the leaves sit unraked on their great lawn, and they can neglect to paint the pillars that make their house a mansion, and they can also talk any way they want. Impervious. Making their own rules, being above the rules. She said actually, from what she knew, everyone had loved William.

"Oh, they did. Even his patients. That's where I first heard of him. A dear friend of mine was his patient. Vivian. She said, Josie, my wonderful doctor, you have to see him; there's never been anyone like him." Mrs. Springer's small brown face bobbed with pleasure. "She was right. Wonderful. Twenty-one years ago, but I remember it like today. That hair, and the big face, and the smile. A prince," Mrs. Springer said.

Nan said nothing.

"He'd come every day; his visits were what kept her going. I'd leave the room, but I'd stand outside and I'd hear his voice and then Vivian's and then his again—so lovely. Don't ask me how he did it. His beeper always ringing, and I know for a fact people were lined up in the hall to waylay him. Dr. Gardiner this, Dr. Gardiner that. But did he cut Vivian short? As if he had all day, he'd sit down for a chat.

And not just about her health either. She loved to travel, and William, it turned out, was a very classy sightseer too —my dear, did you get to travel with him?"

She said in a tight voice that they'd gone for three weeks on a honeymoon.

"Oh, my dear girl, I'm so sorry. I didn't mean—"

"Tell me about William and your friend."

"That's it. They would talk. Museums. Theatre. Restaurants. Didn't matter. Doctor and patient having a civilized conversation—well, you know how it usually is in a hospital?"

Nan said she knew.

"Patient asks a question, and doctor snaps out his answer, and patient is so intimidated she forgets the half dozen things she desperately wants to know—well, not Dr. Gardiner and Vivian. After his visits she'd even look better. She was relaxed, my darling friend. Content. As relaxed and content as someone in that condition can be."

"What was her condition?"

"She was dying. She knew it. Lung cancer with metastases. It had gone to the liver, maybe even the bone. She had six months, seven at the most. She knew, but she didn't want her husband to know she knew—the old story, the strong woman protecting the weak man who isn't worth it, going along with his jolly posing."

"Sad," Nan said. "I mean, that he couldn't be honest."

"That wasn't his only dishonesty. He had a woman. Got one the instant Vivian went even slightly out of commission. She knew about that too, but she never let on. She used to tell me about it. He can marry her the day after I die, she'd say, but I won't die a minute sooner for his convenience, not a minute. I shouldn't tell you all this," Mrs. Springer contentedly said.

"When did that ever stop you, my sweet?" Mr. Springer said.

"Anyhow, I won't tell you who he was."

"See that you don't," he said.

"Well, why shouldn't I? Senator Darnell, he came from one of those Midwest states that begin with *I*, I never can tell one of them from another. They retired him four years ago; some young fellow beat him out, don't you remember? No, I guess you wouldn't. Four years ago, how old were you?—No, don't say it. Thrilling. Imagine being that age, having it all ahead of you."

"My sweet, take it easy."

"Well, Jack Darnell. Big on saving pennies. He was on some committee that bought things for the armed forces; he was always talking about this shop he found that could turn out the buttons on navy uniforms four cents cheaper than the place that made them before."

"Our money he was saving, yours and mine."

"Don't you believe it. He didn't give a hoot about the taxpayer. It was his skinflint personality. All that penny pinching was because he liked to squeeze people down. Make sure nobody was getting a better deal than he was."

"You're just angry because he had another woman."

"You're so right," Mrs. Springer said. "He'd sit there in Vivian's room, that skinflint face and some flowers he got for half price at the corner, and she knew perfectly well he'd make a beeline to that woman the second visiting hours were up."

"I heard she was very nice, actually," Mr. Springer said.

"Isn't that like a man? I heard she was a harpy who was just waiting to get her hands on Jack's money."

"If you'd ever invited them, my sweet, we could have seen for ourselves."

They can go on and on, the rich Mr. and Mrs. Springer

putting on an act. All they need is an audience, and here I am providing it. This cozy sniping that they think is daringly sexy but in truth is merely naughty—the resource of aged children getting their kicks. She looked from one of the complacent wrinkled faces to the other and asked if the sick woman had lived out her six months.

"No, my poor darling Vivian, she died sooner than they thought. Sooner than she wanted. She'd asked me to buy her a bedjacket, blue, Josie, she said, make sure it's blue, the only color I can wear with my skin like this. So I brought her one, plain but nice, and she seemed better. We even walked a little, up and down the hall. And that night I got the phone call. Goodbye, Vivian."

"Did her husband marry that other woman?"

"Oh, yes. I don't think she made him happy."

"What you mean is, you hope she didn't make him happy," Mr. Springer said.

She nodded: his point, indubitably, and this emboldened him to suggest that their visitor had come to hear about William.

"Ah, yes. The wonderful William. Well, Vivian's illness, that was the start of our friendship with him."

"Did he ever tell you about his work?"

"You mean the treatment he was using for Vivian?"

"I was thinking of his, um, outside professional interests."

"Now you remind me, he was working on some research project. Research, that man. How he got the time and energy. He said he had an idea, and I know he was steamed up about it; you could tell from the look on his face. Oh, lord, that face. I think it was something about limiting damage in heart attacks, but he didn't want to go into detail till he'd done more testing."

Nan sat with hands folded on her lap.

"Sounded like one of those intuitions scientists get, and I was interested, naturally—"

"Very natural. You having such a great mind for science, my sweet."

"—I was interested and I asked him to tell us more, and he came one night for dinner, and then another night . . . the upshot was we offered him money from our foundation."

"You offered."

"Bert, sweetheart, I checked with you."

"I was just pointing out who got him off in a quiet corner. Cultivated the contact with the wonderful William."

Still at it: The Springers, spending a morning in amiable contention. She'd turned them toward the past, which was their natural habitat, a place where nothing was subject to censorship or open to contradiction; gaudy and freewheeling, memory could range uninhibited over the territory. If Nan stayed around long enough, Mrs. Springer might even invent a brief fling with William. Or maybe there really was a brief fling, conducted with the furtive concurrence of her husband. Nan sighed and asked what William's response to the money offer had been.

"Anyone who has a serious research project in the works can always use more money. He said he was just starting; to get a really valid result he'd have to get data on many more than the four or five cases he'd followed that far, and for this he'd need a statistician—oh, he was excited, all right. This was his baby, you could see."

"So did you give him money?"

"As it turned out, we didn't. He called one day—it was a few weeks after Vivian died—and said he was dropping the experiment."

"Ah."

"Big pity. I'm sure whatever idea he had, it was an inspired one."

Outside, on the lawn, she saw a mockingbird digging industriously in the rich layer of leaves. "Did he give a reason?"

"None. Just that he wouldn't be needing money. I thought maybe he thought we'd be upset about Vivian, we might hold it against him, but that would've been too ludicrous—a woman slated to die, every medical expert agreed she would die, he couldn't remotely be held responsible."

"Didn't you ask him?"

"We never saw him again. I did invite him a number of times, but for one reason or another he couldn't come— remember, Bert?"

"I have no doubt that you invited him, my sweet."

"We did see him once, just after Vivian died, must have been. It was at some restaurant. He was with a beautiful girl—excuse me, Mrs. Gardiner, I don't mean to—"

"It's all right. I know he took out lots of beautiful girls. Did you happen to get her name?"

"I think he said Marcy something. It was very quick. A snappy hello, nothing else—he didn't seem anxious for anything else. Well. Now you tell me he's dead and someone is going to do a book about him. I don't know that we can tell you any more. Vivian, poor dear, adored him, and so did I, our dream man, but I'm sure you can get the same story from plenty of people."

That gift for easy conquest—she had gotten it. From William's sister, from a colleague, from a rejected head nurse, from an ex-girlfriend, now from this putative benefactor sitting in her moneyed house—from all these diverse sources, in effect, the same story told, the same homage paid. And of course she, Nan, could corroborate it; what was her marriage but another chapter in that saga of innate appeal? William, the mythic hero striding down the corridors of life while on the sidelines every onlooker's heart flutters a little faster.

When she stood, they pressed her to stay. They were going out shortly; perhaps they could show her some of the sights of the city? Or would she like a meeting with her congressman—just take a word from Mr. Springer. Well, then, a private tour of the White House, is she interested in that; they can easily arrange . . . She said no thanks, thinking with what alacrity William, the classy sightseer, would have said yes please.

But she was tired. Who was she kidding: a day in the hospital takes something out of you no matter how chipper you tell yourself you feel on that walk around the block. Besides, she had to prepare for tomorrow's interview. For what she now realized must be tomorrow's interview. All her vaunted skills at listening, her facile sympathy, her air of patient attentiveness that brought out in others their prolific confidences, and the one she was now banking on was a woman whose vocabulary was limited to yes and no.

Chapter
FOURTEEN

AT ONE O'CLOCK, EXACTLY, she got out of the taxi and went up the steps to the house on Maple. No unobstructed admittance this time; she rang the bell and felt herself observed through the peephole before the nurse opened the door. Except she didn't look much like a nurse, this woman who wasn't wearing a uniform, not even a clean apron, just a dishtowel tied around her skirt, and on her feet the kind

of slippers meant for languid shuffling around the house.
She shuffled now. "Yes?"

"I'm a friend of Marcy's. Nan Dunlop. I wonder if I
could see her."

"The sister didn't tell me."

"Well, I wasn't sure. I said sometime this week, maybe
Thursday, I suppose she forgot. . . . Look, I have this puzzle.
Not a real puzzle, just something stroke patients get pleasure doing. See? Just a few pieces, someone using a left
hand can do it easily."

The broad face was still skeptical. "Well, I don't
know . . ."

"Is she having lunch? I could help you with it, cut up her
food or warm it or anything."

Help. The magic word. There was not exactly an invita-
tion to enter, but the slippers did a sliding step along the
floor; the soiled towel moved sideways, so there was room
for Nan to get in. She stood a second in the hall; the same
fetid air, the same slurry sounds from a room where an
invalid must wait longer than she likes to hear the facts:
What's going on, who's there, what are they saying about
me?

Marcy had on the bathrobe and was sitting in her wheelchair, with lunch on a tray in front of her. But nothing to
warm, not even anything to cut up; lunch was two pieces
of bread with a slab of cheese between them, a half tomato,
a glass of milk. And she had eaten it, or at least as much of
it as she wanted; her left hand pushed the plate away with
a fretful little motion.

Nan pulled over another chair. "Marcy, remember me?
I was here the other day. Nan Dunlop. I'm a nurse in New
York."

Did she remember? The green-flecked eyes sent back the
aggressive stare that could mean anything. I'm glad you're

here. Go away and never come back. Save me from that witch inside. How do they expect me to eat this mess? Which?

"You finished lunch? Want another sip of this milk? Well, why don't I move it over here? I brought this puzzle; I thought maybe we could work on it together." She took away the lunch plate; she also picked up the useless claw of a right hand and moved it to the other side of the tray. Then she opened the box. "See, there are these pieces to fit in—looks hard but it really isn't; just takes a little coordination; you have to sort of jiggle each piece until it goes in."

She sat back. God! If someone talked to me in this patronizing way I'd slap her face. But actually Marcy didn't seem to mind; the eyes into which William had stared across a restaurant table revealed not so much anger as bafflement. Someone bringing her a present! Offering to do something in conjunction with her! Her hand did move; it picked up one of the cardboard pieces, let it hover for a second over the scene, and dropped it into the right niche. Nan resisted the temptation to say Good Girl, picked a piece herself, and accomplished a similar feat. Did she act too fast? No, Marcy was making pleased little sounds in her throat; she didn't smile, but her face wore a quizzical expression as she went for her second piece, and then it was Nan's turn again, and then Marcy's, and they were a team. A combine. Marcy and Nan, doing a puzzle together.

The game didn't last long—one failed attempt and the quizzical look lapsed into petulance. Well, what did you expect; you know about their short attention span—grin and move on to the next thing.

The next thing was a pad and pencil that she took out of her pocketbook. "Marcy, would you like to practice writing? I brought these just in case."

"No." A definitive answer at last.

"You mean, no, you don't want to?" And seeing the pained look, "You mean you can't write, is that it? Not with your left hand? Oh, but that hand can do fine—it's hard, but it works; all you need is practice. So now let's start. Your name first. M A R C Y. Remember how the first letter goes?"

She didn't remember. Or she was scared to try. Or she couldn't believe that a pencil held in that unaccustomed left hand could reproduce the precious totem. It didn't matter. With fingers forming an unlikely cradle around the pencil, she went at it, line up, line down, line up, wildly uneven line down, battered but recognizable, and at the sight of the letter, a sound like a laugh came from the tight throat. M for Marcy, set slanting on the yellow paper.

"She has to go to bed now." The woman was at the door.

"Oh, but we're just—"

"This is when I put her to bed. I don't like to do it after I change my clothes."

"I think she'd like to—tell you what. I'll stay on a while after you leave and put her to bed myself. I know how, I can do it. Marcy, would you like to sit up in the chair a little longer?"

An emphatic yes. A yes that was accompanied by a vigorous shake of the head, a bouncing movement of her whole left side.

"She has to be cleaned up and everything." The woman sounded grudging.

Cleaned up . . . precious little had been done until now. The wasted legs put into slippers, the arms coaxed into the faded robe, that was all the cleaning up she could see. "Oh, well, I'll do everything. I'm a nurse, no trouble at all."

"She has to be taken to the bathroom so she can last out till her sister comes."

"She" again: the way they all jumped to inflict the small

indignities. Nan said she'd take care of it, no problem.

The woman untied the towel around her waist. "Bed has to be changed. There's clean sheets in the hall closet."

She's not so dumb, Nan thought. Sees a chance to get the bed made without lifting a finger. She said sure, she was going to do that anyhow. "So you run along whenever you're ready."

"Two o'clock. That's when I'm supposed to leave." The woman left, however, at a quarter of; Nan heard a cupboard door bang in the kitchen, then footsteps from feet that must now be wearing shoes went down the hall, then, "Well, so long now, you be a good girl," drifted into the room, and they were alone.

They were alone, and Marcy was smiling. Not any big salutation of joy, not the kind of liberated curves that can transfigure a face into intimations of its old beauty, but a bona fide assertion of pleasure. Changing the position of those clutching fingers, so now the thumb did most of the work and now a straining forefinger, Marcy worked on the next letter, and the next and the next, and at last she had it. M A R C Y. Her own name inscribed by her own efforts on the page.

"Marcy, hey, that's great. You really should practice, a little every day. Rotten to have to use that hand, but you can do it, plenty of people do—Listen, want me to comb your hair like I did last time? Much easier when you're sitting up. Why don't I wheel you here to the mirror; you can watch, tell me which way you like it? Lord, this beautiful thick hair—up this way? No? Okay, suppose I make the part here, that looks nice, don't you think?"

She did think. The face in the mirror manifested a contentment, almost an exaltation, not just at the location for a part but at this whole, plainly uncustomary activity. Like any woman, Marcy enjoys having her hair combed in front of a mirror. "I've done a lot of this for people who had strokes. I work in New York, well, I guess I told you. Gotham General. A big hospital, I'm on the ninth floor. General and post-surgical cases."

No response from the watchful eyes, but no particular agitation either.

"I got my nursing degree four years ago. I like it, really like the work, I can't imagine doing anything else, but am I ever a wreck when I get home."

In the mirror, that calmly searching gaze: all right so far.

"I suppose they treat us better than they used to, well, fifty years ago, but I still wouldn't exactly call it an easy job. Certainly not for that pay. Well, why am I telling you all this, you know the story, you were a nurse yourself, weren't you?" Testing, testing, and except for an abrupt stiffening around the mouth, a strained look as Marcy shakes her head, there is still no crisis.

"I'm going to massage your right hand—no, don't be scared. I'll do it very gradually; I'll quit the instant it hurts. These poor fingers, doesn't anyone ever try to straighten them?" Stupid question, she can see no one ever tries. "I do this at the hospital too, they say it's important. Keep the joints from stiffening. Gotham General, I mean. That reminds me. There's this doctor there who used to work at your hospital here in Washington. A Dr. Gardiner. William Gardiner. Tall, broad shoulders, I wonder if you—"

But she stopped. She had to stop. Unnecessary to see Marcy's face crumble; it was enough, through her massaging fingers, to feel the jolt of the body so intense it went even through that wasted right hand. "Did I hurt you?" she said smoothly. "I'll quit. These joints are really stiff; I'll get to them another day. A little at a time, okay?"

A little at a time; the only way to conduct this impossible business. She looked at Marcy in the mirror, Marcy whose eyes reflected pained knowledge under their agitated stare, and for a second her impatience was so great she almost yelled out what was on her mind. Just tell me what really went on between you and William—as if her own deep need must overcome Marcy's irreparable impairment.

Well, she'd worked up a list of appropriate questions, questions that could be answered with a yes or no. Did you go out with Dr. Gardiner? Did you stop going out together because you were angry at him? Because he was angry at you? Did he make promises he didn't keep? Did they fire you from Northwest Memorial? Did that firing have anything to do with Dr. Gardiner? Did you know about his research? Is it because of what went on between you and Dr. Gardiner that you refuse to go into a hospital now? And all of them insinuated subtly, one when she brings another puzzle tomorrow, and another as she and Marcy try out a new hairdo the day after, and a third, maybe by then the clincher, when she coaxes Marcy into letting her put on some real clothes and pushes the wheelchair out onto the porch, fresh air and a view of the world at last. . . . Oh, she knew the tactics to soften up someone like Marcy, win her confidence so she was ready to reveal it all.

But not ready yet. "Marcy, don't cry, please, I won't touch your hand again, not this time, I promise. Look, would you like to go back to bed now?" She was working as she talked, plumping a pillow, shaking out blankets, changing sheets that had obviously not been changed for several days. "All right, here we go. Easy does it, move that foot, now the other—you're doing fine. How about I get you a clean nightgown, are they in that drawer?"

They were not in that drawer, it held only a couple of scarves and an old sweater and a portfolio stuffed with papers, but they were in the drawer above; she took one and maneuvered it over the trembling head and useless arm. "Marcy, you rest now." She was resting already; what else could she do between two o'clock when the attendant left and four when her sister came home. Lost hours when she was alone, a prisoner; no, worse than a prisoner, a prisoner at least is master of his own body; during those hours when she was so helpless even the indignities inflicted by others must seem preferable, what panic she must feel, wondering what might happen if there's a fire, a flood, an intruder—of course in that intimidating time Marcy had geared herself to rest.

"Marcy, see you tomorrow, okay?" Silence, the lids down on the fretful eyes, the mouth still. Nan went out, put on her jacket, opened the front door. Then she came back. "Marcy? Marcy, I'm still here." No answer. None while she stood a few minutes in watchful scrutiny, and none when she finally went over to the dresser, opened the bottom drawer, and took out the portfolio. "Marcy . . ." she breathed again, but by then she was out of the room; she was seated at the desk in the living room.

A small desk, its scarred surface not nearly large enough for all the papers; freed from the cardboard case, they tumbled out, some landing on her lap, some rustling like dried leaves to the floor. Was there a classification system, some esoteric arrangement known to only one person, and by her summary handling had she upset it? She picked up the page nearest her hand. A faded newspaper clipping: "At a meeting of the student council, Marcy Drummond was voted Miss Benjamin Franklin High School. Marcy, who has been active in glee club, the Thespian society, and cheerleaders . . ." A scribbled note from someone called Susan: "Marcy, guess who's wild for you? My brother Pete, isn't that a scream. He's dying to ask you to the game, but he doesn't have the nerve." A nursing school graduation program: "Highest honors to Elaine Stass, Marcy Drummond, and Margaret Price for their . . ."

No, there was not a classification system. But there was a kind of theme, the one imposed by tribute and adulation. Yellowed, creased, partly illegible, these papers defined someone possessed of youth, talent, beauty, luck. A letter from Robert: ". . . will never forget that day with you on the beach." One from Lester: "Well, baby, they just made me head of the sales division. I know you wouldn't want to live in Carson City forever, but if you would consider it for a couple of years . . ." A note on blue paper from someone who signed herself Lucille B: "I am sending these roses for my mother, who will always remember the devoted care and amazing skill with which you took care of her after the operation."

All these exercises in tender remembering. Did Marcy ask for this portfolio from time to time; did she fumble at it with her awkward left hand, sorting out the futile solicitations? Was she sorry she turned down Lester and the brave new start in Carson City?

A card from Pete, who has obviously steeled himself to blow his own horn: "To my best girl on her twentieth birthday." A half dozen letters in a manila envelope: "Joe and I were grieved to hear the sad news about your father . . . all know, Marcy, how much he meant . . . deepest sympathy . . . condolence . . ." Letter in an envelope postmarked California: "Guess you heard the great news about the baby. Well, Sis, here's the reason for the letter. We want to name her Marcy, in hopes she'll turn out a beauty like her aunt." Small white card signed, simply, E: "Wear them and think of me."

Them. Flowers? Furs? Jewelry? Nan held the card between intense fingers, as if to decipher it as she'd tried to decipher Marcy's anguished stare. She knew the rules: guilt is supposed to filter in. Like anyone prying into another's life, you're intruding. Trespassing on premises not open to the public. Making unauthorized use of personal data.

But it was her data too: along with the vague regret there was the distinct sense of identification. Sitting here with these pastel souvenirs, she was remembering her own importunate lovers, the day she was elected Miss Central High School, her triumphs in a cheerleader's rippling skirt. "You remind me of someone I knew long ago"—no wonder he'd said it. You and me, Marcy: William's women.

Except she couldn't afford to indulge in that kind of facile nostalgia. She had to quit, after all, by three thirty, so she could get the papers back into the portfolio and the portfolio into its drawer before Linda arrived home at four o'clock. Would she be able to read everything? Yes, if she kept going she'd be able to.

Another petition from Lester: "Carson City isn't the worst, we could have fun, baby, I swear . . ." A valentine —"Today and every day"—signed Al. Another valentine signed, obscurely, the Twins. A letter from Brenda Lambert: "Marcy, don't mind what they say, we all know you were the best, absolutely the snappiest nurse they ever had on Cavendish Six." Well, this was more like it: no date and no envelope, but Brenda might just turn out to have something, and she noted the address, which was on Kalorama Road, N.W.

She put Brenda on the done pile, which looked infinitesimal compared to the papers still sprawled across the desk. On second thought, she might not finish today. Another session, at least, until from out of these yellowed leaves she pulled whatever was relevant. She passed up two envelopes that held report cards, and a bill from an orthodontist— even a stunner like Marcy can need some assists—and then she felt her insides wrenched as if someone were shaking them, because the next letter was signed Tad: "Marcy dear. It's a devilish time for you, I know, but try not to be too upset. What should you do about what we talked about yesterday? Do nothing. Remember, everyone is entitled to one big error in a lifetime."

She read it again. And again. First time she'd seen Tad's handwriting. Not the big plain-dealing letters of William's, rather the typical physician's scrawl that doesn't bother to go in for the cursive niceties, but she could read it. Devilish time for you. One big error . . . She could read it fine. Had there already been the instance of mixing up the medication that Linda mentioned? Was Marcy then slipping into what they euphemistically termed a nervous breakdown? Had she received notice that the hospital was letting her go? Someone who had gone from the snappiest nurse Cavendish Six ever had to one who was not deemed competent to hand out pills, the glee-club member, the cheerleader, the beloved of Lester and Al and Pete and the twins and of course William, let's not forget William . . . that woman with the green-flecked eyes and high cheekbones was a presence here in the living room, the sense of her was so strong that when Nan heard the front door open and footsteps in the hall, she didn't move.

Besides, what good would moving be? No way she could possibly sweep up these papers and get them back in their assigned place before someone came in; that posture of innocence had been forfeited.

Someone had come in now. "What do you think you're doing?" Almost the same words Linda had used the last time.

"I'm very sorry. I should have asked you."

"You should not have asked me; I don't like to hear dumb requests."

When she stood, the clipping from the school newspaper fell to the floor: Marcy Drummond voted Miss Benjamin Franklin High School.

"So that's all you wanted the whole time. To spy on us. Steal our property."

"Listen, I'm not taking anything, of course I'm not, I'll put it all back the way I—"

"Don't touch anything. Keep your hands off that desk." In her gray schoolteacher's suit, her rayon blouse with bow, Linda stood unmoving in the doorway. "A common thief. Breaking into people's homes."

"I didn't break in, that's crazy, I—"

"I know exactly how you wheedled your way in. Have this puzzle. Want to help cut up her food." Linda's face twisted as she mimicked Nan's words.

So that was why Linda was here, an hour ahead of schedule. Imagine. That woman with the run-down slippers and dishtowel belt who acted as if she couldn't care less. "We don't require any help," Linda said.

She looked down for a second at the scattered papers. Under a piece of tissue was a dried corsage—sent by Lester? by Pete?—she had not noticed before. "You do need help," she burst out. "She's a mess, honestly, lying there day after day, no one training her speech or helping to strengthen her muscles or exercise her hand. Even walking, she could manage a lot better than she does; her leg movement isn't bad at all; if someone would just stand next to her while she . . ."

Enough! Linda's plain features were distorted as though a hand had come down and twisted them out of shape. "Don't criticize the way I take care of my sister. Do not criticize it," Linda said.

"Linda, I'm sorry. I know how hard, how excruciating, really—"

"You're a fine one." With her eyes glaring and her mouth pulled up at one side, Linda looked more like Marcy—the Marcy who lay in helpless fury inside, not the one projected by violet memory. "All those big offers of help, the sweet little nurse. You only did it so you could get something out of her."

Well, it's true, isn't it? What else was it all for, the puzzles, the pad, the bed-making, the murmured flattery in front of a mirror, except a calculated effort to induce a sick woman to divulge her secrets?

No, it's not true. Because secrets or not, if she were the one taking care, Marcy would not be lying with hair tangled, muscles unused, eyes glazed with emptiness.

"Listen, could we close Marcy's door?"

"What difference does it make?"

"Well, I don't want her to—"

"To know that you're here to spy on her? That that's the reason for all the sweet stuff?"

"Right," Nan said tightly. "I really wish she didn't have to know."

"Doesn't matter what she thinks," Linda said. "You're never going to see her again."

"Linda, I told you how important—"

"I don't want to hear."

"It's my whole life. I'm accused of having done something; Marcy's the only one who can—"

"You keep on like this, and I'll call the police. I'll tell them what you did. Reading the mail of someone who's helpless, the police won't think that's such a nice idea."

Linda was absolutely right. Those authorities who thought there were still unanswered questions about sleeping pills; no way she could explain to them what she was up to here. "Okay, I understand about these papers; I never should have. But please let me talk to Marcy. Not today, some other time, just to ask her a few—"

"Get out," Linda said, and under the gray suit, her shoulder performed a small, peremptory movement.

"You can sit there with us. Hear every single thing I—"

"I think I'll call them right now," Linda said and moved toward the phone.

"No, don't. I'm going. But can I ask you a question? Without your getting all—I mean why? Why are you so opposed to my talking to your sister?"

"Because I'm in charge and I say so," Linda said. "Now get going."

How readily she fell into the squalid speech patterns. There she was, a woman dressed to project ladylike dignity, a schoolteacher, uttering these crude ultimatums. Did she have some valid reason why her sister must remain mute? Or had she simply been caught up in the imperatives of the scene: helpless invalid, blasphemous intruder, sister to the rescue?

Linda was still standing with her hand on the phone. A confrontation with the police—the last thing she was in shape to handle just now. Get out, Linda said, and she got, walking around the desk, keeping a fastidious straight line between the wing chair and the couch. At the doorway she paused; she and Linda were within a few inches of each other, the gray-flecked eyes staring impassively into hers. Maybe, after all, it was the way Linda acted in the classroom. Johnny, down to the principal's office. Mary, I'm in charge and I say so. No, Susan, you can't take the test late, you know I don't like to hear dumb requests.

"Don't think you're coming back here ever. Mrs. Moss will know not to let you in. And don't try any tricks. Next time it won't be Marcy waiting but a man in blue uniform."

Hear that, Marcy old girl? No more puzzles, no more delectable sessions of hair-combing in front of the mirror.

She looked in at the sickroom as she went by. That rigid face lying motionless on the pillow—did she hear everything? Will she think I betrayed her? Did I betray her?

"Keep going. We don't need you." Linda was still at it, pulling rank, trading on that flimsy authority, and like a misbehaving pupil who has no wish to be sent to the principal, Nan opened the door and went out on the porch where she and Marcy after all would not sit, and down to the indifferent quiet of Maple Avenue.

Chapter

FIFTEEN

FAILURE, NAN THOUGHT. Once it starts, there's no turning around; let a life get on the skids, and it stays there, downhill all the way. Downhill faster if it starts from the top. Because those early triumphs don't help, the estimable record doesn't help, even a disproportionate allotment of good looks and talent doesn't help. Going down in the world: it's a tag that says infectious, don't try to help, stay away or you might catch it too.

That was what she thought, anyhow, after a couple of days of checking up on Marcy, following the tortuous course that had led from a snappy nurse in a prestigious hospital to an atrophied body in a rumpled bed.

Brenda Lambert:

Yes, of course I remember Marcy, how could you not remember? I mean, it really can get you up a wall. You think if someone like that could go wrong, there's nothing left to count on.

I'm not the only one. I bet if you stopped any nurse who worked on that floor. Even the patients. It's the truth. After they got out, they used to send her things. Flowers, nuts, cards, I don't know what all. Thank you for taking such good care of me or my mother or my aunt or I don't know who all. Maybe you don't know about hospitals? A little? Well, patients sending presents to a nurse, that's not the routine, believe me. It's more the other way. Like my husband, he was in last month for a few days, not even anything serious, just his back went out, the doctor said try traction. Well, you wouldn't catch him sending anyone flowers. When he came home, what he said was never again. He said the way they treat you there, it isn't human.

So Marcy, someone like that, well, of course I remember. I mean, that girl, she didn't just take good care, she'd make patients feel good care was what they deserved. I mean, she'd talk to them. No, that's not right either. She'd let them talk to her. You'd go by some room where she was working, giving a bath, say, or dressing the incision, and there was the sound of someone talking. Jabber, jabber, jabber. That kind of contented noise. You think that's silly? Oh, I thought because you sort of jumped. Marcy's theory was it makes them feel better if they think someone is interested. It gives them an incentive. I don't know, she must have been doing something right. I remember once I was wheeling this patient down from post-op, he was still groggy, you ask me they don't keep them there half long enough. So he gets out of the elevator, he doesn't know which end is up, but he knows enough to say Miss Drummond, why can't Miss Drummond come?

You see what I mean. For someone like that to fall apart. Fall from grace, my mother used to say. What's that you heard? Mixed up medications? Gave people the wrong dose? Well, maybe she did. I can't say I ever saw it, it's hard to believe a nurse like Marcy, nursing just built into her, but I know it's what they said. And it really is true, I guess, if you have a terrible burden pressing on you, you'll do anything. What burden? Oh, she never told me. I only know that much because I walked into the linen closet one day when she was standing there crying. It's all on me, she said, crying to beat the band. All on me. What? Oh, I don't know, I'm sure, I just said could I get her water or anything, I wouldn't dare ask any questions.

No, we weren't really friends. Goodness, I was just starting. Miss Dimwit from South Carolina, new in the big city. I didn't have the nerve to eat with them, I fainted if one of them had coffee with me in the nurses' lounge. Besides, I wasn't even an RN then, I didn't take my boards till a couple of years later. Practical nurse—lowest of the low. You can't imagine how it is in a hospital, everyone taking it out on the guy below. Surgeon dumps on the general doctor, and doctor dumps on the resident, and the resident —oh, you do know. Well, okay, Marcy wasn't fixing to confide in me. A nobody from nowhere.

Where she is now? I don't know, I'm sure, why don't you ask the hospital? Or one of her friends, there was another nurse, Gail, I think. Besides, I'm not even sure. And I have to be careful and all, my husband working for HUD. Oh, it's an acronym, in Washington everything's an acronym; sometimes I think we're all acronyms. It means Housing and Urban Development. So his being a civil servant and all, I don't like. I mean it's not nice to spread slander. Well, if you promise you won't, one of the doctors told me—look, it might not even be true—he said they saw her one night, it was about four years later, could have been someone else. I mean they saw her at this topless place called Varsity.

One of those joints down on Fourteenth Street. Sure, I know what you mean, people will say anything. Well, it probably wasn't even Marcy, the nurse I knew, believe me she wasn't like that. Or maybe fifteen years ago, those places were different from what they are now. Oh, sure, I agree, funny things do happen.

Tim Fitzhugh, Manager of Varsity:

Drummond? Marcy Drummond? Never heard of her. Yes, of course I'm sure, I remember them all. Sixteen years back? Shit, I remember twenty-one, twenty-two years back. The work I put into those girls, I damn well ought to remember. Oh, sure, some of them do that, fake names, why shouldn't they? Just last month police were here looking for this girl, name of Susan Ash, they had a bench warrant out for her, only the name she went under here—

Not like that? They all tell you they're respectable. I'm a very respectable girl, I never did anything like this before, I just have to do this because my father died, the mortgage is due, my brother needs an operation. What? A nurse? Shit, we have them, they were bank clerks, secretaries, actresses, even schoolteachers. Fact. This schoolteacher's here now, she got up at six-thirty every morning so high-school girls could learn Latin conjugations. So now she gets up at six-thirty at night so hayseeds from Squeedunk can learn what's what in the nation's capital. Shit, even me. Know what I used to be? A ballet dancer. I even did choreography. This routine I put on here—kick, step, kick, step —you don't think this is what I aimed at. You ever see our act? No, I guess you wouldn't. So our ballet group, very heavy stuff. Pyrotechnics, they'd say. Ingenuity. Magical atmosphere. Shit, you can't eat pyrotechnics. Like I said, I'd like to help you—Hey, nurse did you say? Comes to me now. We did have one. This would be, I don't know, fifteen, sixteen years back. Funny. She didn't say she was a nurse, didn't say much of anything—way we found out, one of the girls got sick one night, food poisoning I think it was, and your friend, if she was your friend, took care of her till the ambulance came. Oh, green eyes, I remember that. Nice reddish-brown hair. Good-looking girl, I have to give her that, but too skinny. I told her, eat something, what's the good of showing it if you don't have what to show? Mary Diamond—yeah; comes to me now. I know it is, funny how they do that, make up some new name and it's practically the same as their old. Like they have to cling to it, they can't bear to strike out with something new.

Oh, she did all right. No house afire, those skinny breasts, but she worked out. Conscientious, I'll give her that. No, what happened was some people she knew came in, I think they were from the hospital. No trouble, just a bunch of young doctors having theirselves a night out, but she got all uptight. After the first number she said she had a headache, she didn't want to go back out—couldn't I? I couldn't. Shit, you can't pick and choose. You're not ready to handle it, find another job, I tell them. No sweat, they can keep all their clothes on doing checkout in a supermarket.

No, how should I know? No, wait, maybe I do know. There was an old fellow used to come around, I heard she was working for him. Search me, I don't know what she'd do for him. Well, maybe I do know. Oh, Merrill something. Or something Merrill. You know that big furniture store, Formost Furniture, I think it's called? Out on Wisconsin, third alphabet? That was his place. Or maybe I heard wrong—no guarantees, I'm not saying anything. Something eating that girl, I wasn't sorry to see her go. They're none of them that dependable, but she was worse. I asked her when she was leaving why she wouldn't go back to nursing, all she said was hospitals, that's all shit. Well, you

see her, tell her Tim doesn't bear any grudges. Got that?
Tell her I send my best.

Loretta Merrill:

Marcy Drummond? Yes, of course. Worked for my
brother Henry, how could I forget. What? Oh, she was a
companion. He was an old man, well, sixty-nine, that may
not be exactly old, but what with his arthritis, and no
longer able to get around as he once—

What she did?—well, you know. I never had a companion myself, can't say I ever felt the need to, but I can
imagine. Whatever a companion does for an elderly man
with some disabilities. Wrote his letters, I daresay. Accompanied him when he went for a drive. Supervised the staff.
There was a cook and some cleaning people, but she—
That's correct. General duties.

Oh, yes, she seemed a nice young woman. Nervous type,
but pleasant enough. Good manners. Pleasing features, except for that twitch. I can't say I knew her very well, not
well enough, for instance, to advise her to see a doctor for
that little facial irregularity, though I often did think.
However, every time I came, things were in presentable
shape. Rooms clean, help content, meals served regularly.
Oh, five years, give or take a few months. Or did she stay
with him for six years? In any case, she left a year before
he died. I remember his saying he was looking around for
someone else, but I don't think he ever—

Yes, he had retired by then. Turned the business over to
associates, though of course he still had a good income. Yes.
Enterprising. Creative. Built it up by himself. I don't, as it
happens, admire that kind of furniture, but I can see. Yes,
young people, naturally, they really do seem to.

Close? Henry and I? I can't say that I. I lead a busy life.
Gardening, that steady delight, I don't let my own little
disabilities—and then my needlepoint, and my various

Boards. Oh, the Mellon, and a children's home here in the District, and also a school for handicapped out near Arlington, you wouldn't believe what good work. Well, Henry, different directions, let's say. I always took an interest, an older sister, only natural. For his birthday I gave him a membership in the Smithsonian, some very worthwhile series of lectures, but I can't say that he. And of course, his need for a companion, I was not aloof, not a bit. In fact, I suggested a very nice woman I happened to know. On the staff of the handicapped school, but looking for something rather less. A responsible woman in her sixties. Or when he found her unsuitable, I called a friend at one of the universities. Always plenty of young men, reputable students looking for a little extra money who will gladly. Well, Henry had his life and I had mine; there's no accounting. That young woman—what did you say her name was again? Yes. Miss Drummond. Indeed, I don't pretend to judge. His wife never talked, I give her credit. When she divorced him, she revealed nothing that could possibly. And I didn't press her. Definitely not. But that kind of pathology is not exactly a closed book, is it, we are all sophisticated adults, we recognize that when a man manifests an exaggerated interest in certain subjects, that is to say, when he is morbidly dependent on that kind of outlet rather than on the so-called normal ones.

No, I'm sorry, I never saw her after that. No ill will, certainly not, but there was no occasion. I believe Glady did. Oh, Glady Johnson, she'd been in charge of downstairs cleaning. She came to Henry's funeral, very considerate of her. Those women, time is money, you know, to take out half a day. She said she'd seen Miss Drummond several times, she was not in good health. I can't say I was surprised. When a young woman chooses to squander her attributes in that fashion. Well, good reasons, no doubt. It's not for us to judge, don't you agree?

Glady Johnson:

Do I remember Marcy, poor lamb? How could I forget? That beautiful girl, when I think how she's lying there— No, I have me a handkerchief, thanks.

What was she like? Dreamboat, that's what. That face, you'd look at it and your heart, I mean it, would beat a little faster. Come to think of it, Miss, she looked a little bit like you. Don't blush. Something about the shape of the cheeks, and the expression. Okay, maybe you're right, but just for a second I thought I saw. Anyhow, Marcy, she was a picture. The kind you don't meet up with often in a job like mine. And brains too, that girl. So don't expect me to help you, I never could figure it myself. What was she doing, her looks and brains, working for a dirty old man like that?

Oh, sure. All he was. We all knew it. The way he talked, right in front of us help, no respect at all. Sometime if he was giving a big party, they'd have me in to wait on table, and I'd hear him. The kind of jokes you'd blush to have your own husband tell you in the dark. And there he was, right at his own table, saying words like that in front of mixed company, honest to God, I'd want to drop the platter.

Well, maybe that's what they have to do, those men who are no good in bed. Tell dirty jokes and look down the girls' dresses and pinch their behinds. All they can do. Well, sure, what else do you think he wanted her for? Come in and sit on my lap, Marcy. Come in and dry my back, my hands are so stiff. Sick? That one? Sick my foot, he never had a doctor till that heart attack that took him off. Sick in the head, that's what. Him and his dirty movies that he made her sit next to him and look at. Oh, sure, every night, right after dinner. And the projector right there in the living room— you'd think he'd have the decency to hide it. Companion? That's what they called it? Any daughter of mine says she wants to be companioning, I'll put her over my lap and whip her.

Yes. High time too. Happiest day of my life when she came and said she was quitting. I figured maybe now she'd make something of herself. But I don't know, maybe it ruins you, the years with a man like that. Something shows. Like an infection, written all over you. Nothing can go right. No, she never latched on to anything steady. I'd see her once in a while—she was living with her schoolteacher sister by then—and it was always the same story. The job didn't pay right. The work didn't pan out. The boss started fooling around. Yes, bad luck all the way, poor darling.

And her health wasn't too good. Even that funny little blink she did with her eyes, anyone could see something was wrong. But would she go to a doctor? Stubborn, that one. She didn't need a doctor, nothing a doctor could do. So if she'd gone to a doctor back then, would it have saved her from getting that stroke, would it? I just plain don't know.

How do I know about it? I was there, that's how. I took care of her. Right. Eight to six, every day. The sister called and said would I come? I told them, it's not Glady Johnson you need, a case like this, get a real nurse; what do I know about stroke? But the sister insisted. She said they couldn't afford a real nurse. Besides, she said Marcy wants you. Standing right next to the bed, it's what she said. She likes you, she really wants you.

I think she did. Anyhow, I did my best. Even got me a book that told how to take care of people like that. Not like a trained nurse, I don't pretend I was as good as that, they must have all kinds of tricks. But I cleaned her up nice and sweet. Kept her room neat. Combed her hair. Tried to cheer her up, poor darling. As much as you can cheer up someone like that. There were days she'd lie there crying and crying, nothing I could say or do. I don't know, it just doesn't seem right. You can't tell me she wasn't a good girl at heart. So just for rubbing that old man's naked back and sitting next to him at those movies, it seems like too much punishment, it really does.

Oh, six months. Yes. June till right before Christmas. Then the sister said they were getting someone else. I didn't mind; by then I was starting to feel not so great myself. I didn't know, but three months later, that's when they had to take off this leg. Besides, if it was going to help that poor girl— Someone trained, like the sister said. How could they afford it all of a sudden? Oh, well, that lawyer came and said this person was giving her all that money. No, I don't know the name, the sister took him into the living room, me puttering back and forth to the kitchen I couldn't hardly hear anything. Just how this person, the donor they called him, he admired Marcy long ago and now he was giving this money and Marcy could have all the care she needed. No, definitely I didn't hear a name, and the sister didn't know either. I heard her ask, and the lawyer said he wasn't—authorized, is that the word? But couldn't have been old man Merrill, he was dead by then. So some other rich admirer, but I never knew of any; if he admired her all that much I wish he'd have come earlier and took her away from that place.

No, I can't very well go to see her, laid up like this. Besides, the sister says don't come. She says seeing me like this, it would just make Marcy feel worse. Maybe she's right. Maybe it wouldn't be good for Marcy, her old friend having to be carried in. But I sure hope they're treating her right, those trained nurses and all. So if you see her, tell her I'm thinking of her. Will you do that? You promise? Tell her Glady will love her always.

Chapter
SIXTEEN

IT WAS LATE AFTERNOON when she left Glady Johnson's. The rain had stopped, and she felt the need to walk. All this participating in someone else's life gets to you, she thought; it leaves you feeling smothered, as if on a hot summer day you were enveloped in a heavy overcoat. And you can't just throw the coat off. As she walked along, Marcy's afflictions encased her, pressed in on her, so she was the one jiggling her breasts in the front row of the Varsity, she was stroking the hand of that old man while the blue movies unrolled, she lay still, an inarticulate hulk, while a sister gave voice to her wishes. But if you appropriate another woman's suffering, wouldn't you suppose you could also then be privy to the events that caused it? Doesn't that seem a fair exchange? Well, it turns out not to work that way. For all the profound and painful ways in which she's joined to Marcy, the gaps in information persist. The facts she's been searching for aren't revealed to her. Marcy, her twin, but there's no breakthrough in communication.

She walked faster, conscious that people were looking at her. Boys in the doorway of a boarded-up store, an old man hunched against a wall, two women pushing baby carriages, all fixing her with the same truculent inquiry— maybe this wasn't the kind of street where a strange woman walked alone. She hailed a taxi—what a city for getting taxis. "Where to, lady?" She couldn't say she wanted a phone booth, though that was the truth; sitting back heavily—the smothering overcoat still weighed her down—she gave the address of her motel.

Better that way. She was in no shape to deal with the whims of a public telephone. She could sit like a lady in her own living room, that anonymous background that was beginning to feel like home, while she called Victor's law firm in New York and told who she was and asked did they have a Washington office?

"Just a minute." It was more than a minute, and the ready anger spurted up. She might have known. Victor had them programmed, an alarm to go off if Nan Gardiner called, no help whatsoever to be given. But the voice came back and gave not just the name of the firm but its address and phone number, as well as the name of the attorney— Cyrus Depew—who handled their Washington matters. Did he ever do any legal work for Dr. Gardiner? Oh, she wasn't in a position to answer that, but surely if Mrs. Gardiner called him.

Mrs. Gardiner did call. No, Mr. Depew couldn't see her right away this afternoon; no, unfortunately he was also busy tomorrow and the next day. . . . An emergency? Life and death? Well, just a minute. A closer approximation to a minute this time: If it was so important, Mr. Depew would fit her in at nine-thirty tomorrow.

She said thank you very much. Then she hung up and said I can't stand it. Nine-thirty tomorrow—more than sixteen hours. How does anyone stand it? That exercise in suspense, it's what she most marvels at when she sees people go through it at the hospital. She's made a study of all the tactics. Some sit with glazed eyes in the waiting room; some attack anything in print, a menu, the brochure on hospital regulations, yesterday's newspaper, anything;

some stride zombielike up and down the hall; some do what the doctor says, that unrealistic advice delivered in the professionally hearty voice just to go out and have yourself a sandwich and a plate of soup because you can't accomplish anything sitting here. She can't imagine going out or even moving; immobility is her tactic, as if her steadfast tenancy of this green chair were mystically conjoined to Mr. Depew's promise to see her tomorrow morning.

But presently she did get up; she surprised herself by the dinner she was able to eat; she even managed a few hours' sleep against the thudding of that inner debate. It was William who gave the money. It wasn't William. Was. Wasn't. And suppose Mr. Depew didn't see her after all— he had a heart attack overnight, his car broke down, his house burned, his wife had a baby.

Next morning Mr. Depew would see her. "Mrs. Gardiner? Yes, he's expecting you. If you'll come this way."

This way was a shorter distance to traverse than to Victor's office, only three doors to pass, fewer pictures and a less imposing display of paneling along the walls. Good. A small office, he'd have an easier time remembering. Besides, William—who could ever forget William? Mr. Depew was waiting to shake her hand, and she thought, of course he didn't forget; he too had the vision of that expansive face, the broad shoulders, the whole aura of confident splendor.

"Then you did know my husband?"

"Oh, yes. Remarkable man. I can't tell you how sorry."

He sounded sorry. A prominent lawyer, she knew, had to be adept at pulling out the appropriate words, but the grieving tone sounded sincere; sympathy sat with conviction on the heavy-set face.

"And you handled his Washington business?"

"Whatever business he had in Washington, that's correct; I was the one to handle it."

She felt herself trembling. She'd been so eager, counting minutes, impelling the elevator to go faster, silently berating the receptionist for her languid walk down the hall, and now she couldn't get it out. She put her pocketbook down and picked it up. She wasted a precious minute telling him again how much she appreciated his making time for her. But eventually she managed. What she wanted to know, what it was really important for her to know, was whether at some time—it must have been, oh, three, three and a half years ago—her husband had made a gift of money to a woman called Marcy Drummund.

She hadn't looked at him while she was talking, but now she met the mild gaze from his puffy eyes. "Of course if your husband gave someone a present, there's no reason I should know anything about it."

"Oh, but this was different. I mean, whoever gave it acted through a lawyer; that much I do know."

"I see." Mr. Depew sat with folded hands. "Well, even in a transaction drawn up by an attorney, it's customary for the recipient to know the donor's name."

"But that's the whole point, there was nothing customary about this business. The donor—" What a horrid word, donor. So unsuited to William's free open nature—"Well, the donor never came around. The lawyer attended to everything."

"May I ask who your source is for all this, Mrs. Gardiner?"

It had occurred to her on the way over that he might ask this—now she was sorry she hadn't prepared a better answer. Except wasn't the truth always the best? She explained in brief about Glady Johnson.

He didn't frown; his face kept its courteously interested expression while he asked why she didn't go directly to the recipient.

Another explanation—Marcy's sickness, Linda's necessary assumption of care. "But from what I'm told, Linda, that is, the sister, never knew where the money came from either."

"In short, it was the intention of this hypothetical donor that his identity not be mentioned."

She said that must have been the case.

"However, assuming it was Dr. Gardiner, you would like *me* to mention it."

"Mr. Depew, I—"

"You realize, of course, Mrs. Gardiner, that the relationship between an attorney and his client is a confidential one."

She wanted to say, why'd you shake hands with me so nicely, fit me into your busy day, all that heavy cordiality, if it was just going to lead to this cat-and-mouse routine?

"Oh, I understand. Goodness. I should hope so. But I'm his wife."

"You weren't his wife in the period you're inquiring about. Three years ago, did you say?"

"Then you mean he did give it?"

"I hope nothing I've said leads you to draw either that conclusion or its opposite. All I've tried to point out is that according to the code of legal ethics, I'm not at liberty to discuss anything that went on between Dr. Gardiner and me three years ago. You'd expect the same consideration if you were the client," he added with irrelevant solicitude.

"Oh, of course. I understand," she said again. What was all this? She understood nothing. She stood up and walked over to the window. Outside, beyond the nearby roofs, was a building whose rounded outlines she recognized. Not a museum, not any of the government buildings, but surely she'd seen that domed top commemorated in pictures over and over.

"Mr. Depew, let's start over. Maybe I gave the wrong

impression. I don't want to find out anything discreditable. About William! My God, of course not. This would be his having done something generous. Decent."

Mr. Depew inclined his head. Does that mean she's making progress?

"Or just frivolous curiosity, wanting to check up on someone he knew in his past, a woman he may have gone with—I swear it's nothing like that."

"Unfortunately, your motives don't come into this, Mrs. Gardiner."

"Or maybe I didn't explain how sick this Marcy Drummond is. A stroke—you can't talk, you can't even move by yourself, your whole right side—the worst. And William hadn't seen her for years. Fifteen or twenty, just about. So the fact of his giving her money—"

"Of course if you know he gave her money, you don't need corroboration from me."

"All I know is someone did, I think it was William, all the signs point to it, but unless I can be sure—oh, I can't believe this is so difficult." She stood again. Don't panic. He's just acting with the reserve proper to a member of the bar faced with someone he's never seen before. But once you approach him right, a girl with an authentic claim on his attention, and pretty besides— "Mr. Depew, I wish you would tell me."

"I wish I could."

"Suppose you don't say anything. Just nod your head. Yes or no." Like Marcy. Vocabulary reduced to the two seminal words.

"I'm devoutly sorry, Mrs. Gardiner."

"There just could be a criminal element."

"If the police serve me with a subpoena, of course I'll have to tell them anything I know." Mr. Depew spoke with gentle irony.

Well, the police. She could picture it. Linda won't let me

pump her sister for information, Nan says. Very interesting, say the police. And you say she's resentful because she found you reading her private mail after you had used deceit to get into their home?

She watched him fold his hands. He wasn't just speaking off the top of his head. Meetings with others in the firm, consultations with the New York office, must have followed her phone call. Like the nursing supervisor who suggested that the hospital would be better off without Nan Dunlop, he had the weight of collective wisdom behind him; it was what enabled him to sit there with such serene firmness.

"Mr. Depew, I admit, I wasn't honest with you."

His face registered a discreet alert.

"Not wholly honest, that is. I said I was interested in finding out, as if it were simply a matter of tracking down my husband's past. The truth is—well, I guess you know I inherited William's money; you must have heard."

He bent his head: a man showing respect.

"So much money . . . I feel, no, not guilty, of course not. But it's more than I need, more than I can possibly spend, I'd like to give away some of it in a way that strings along with William's wishes. There's a society that does research into pulmonary and cardiac disease in New York, I know he was interested; well, that's one answer. But I'd like some gifts of a more, well, personal nature too." How is she doing? No hint from the fleshy mouth and shaded eyes. "So now if I can get confirmation about this woman, was she someone William considered worthy . . ."

"I really regret that legal ethics won't permit me to—"

"I'm not asking for the *amount* of money that—"

"Mrs. Gardiner, there's no way—"

"What I mean is, William would have *wanted* you to tell me."

Mr. Depew turned his puffy gaze toward the window and said unfortunately he couldn't make that assumption the basis for his action.

Someone at the door? A newcomer might be a help, two of them with the power to overrule that collective decision. Besides, as a woman she might be better off with two adversaries, their prepossessing weight serving to underline her frail appeal. "Look, is there another lawyer in the office, he might—"

"I'm the senior partner of this firm, Mrs. Gardiner." He said it affably, unassertively, but within her everything was shaking. She knew it was no time for her to talk; the suddenly furious beating of her heart was enough to signal caution.

"It's Victor, isn't it? Victor Hemmings. He got to you when he heard I called. He told you whatever I wanted not to give an inch."

"I don't need Mr. Hemmings to instruct me in—"

"Oh, you make me sick, both of you. All that about ethics. What's ethical, I'd like to know, about keeping a woman from knowing something her own husband did? Something big-hearted and decent. And no one would be hurt; just the opposite, there's a chance I'd be doing something good. I mean, it might be important. Important to a couple of lives, but that factor doesn't enter your computer, does it—no, it's too jammed up with footnotes and precedents; you don't even hear what I'm trying to say. Oh, you should be ashamed, standing there like a robot, handing out all that stuff about ethics and confidence. . . ."

"Anything wrong?" Another lawyer at the door after all. Victor, his long sober face looking even longer and more sober because he'd plainly heard at least part of what she'd been saying. Well, things couldn't be any worse; now their impossible dialogue would be an impossible threesome.

Mr. Depew spoke promptly—maybe he was relieved to pass the buck. "Mrs. Gardiner would like to know whether her husband made a monetary gift several years ago to a certain Miss Drummond. I explained that if I did carry out such a commission for Dr. Gardiner, it would be subject to the confidentiality between lawyer and client. However, this is less than satisfying to Mrs. Gardiner because she's inclined to give money to this same Miss Drummond, and she wants to ascertain whether such a gift would coincide with wishes held by Dr. Gardiner during his lifetime."

Fair enough. It was not exactly the words she'd have chosen, but she had to admit it was a fair presentation of her case. All her arguments and pleas and passionate exhortations boiled down to this one staid paragraph. So it was now on Victor, Victor who was quiet for a long minute while Mr. Depew wiped his face with his handkerchief, and somewhere a phone rang, and someone opened the door and by the expressions on their faces was advised to close it quickly.

"Well, if Mrs. Gardiner wants to donate money to someone," Victor said, "I think she's wise to try to find out what her husband's inclinations were in that direction." He was agreeing. Dear God, Victor was actually saying yes. He was saying it, of course, in the chilly voice he considered appropriate for parlance with her, his face wore its usual look of flat animosity, but what did she care—he was telling Mr. Depew to give her the facts; he even went on to say that he felt this was a case in which a woman's need for edification overrode their natural instinct for confidentiality.

They both were looking at her, and she nodded. "Yes, I do want to give money to Marcy Drummond." She felt an odd relief that there was an element of at least partial truth in her statement.

Mr. Depew sighed and said in that case he could apprise

Mrs. Gardiner of the fact that three years ago Dr. Gardiner had made a gift, quite a sizable gift, to one Marcy Drummond.

"How sizable?"

"Two hundred thousand dollars."

She heard Victor's breath go out in a long exhalation, but she didn't look up; she stared at the carpet. Maybe if she didn't interject herself, they would go on more freely; Mr. Depew would tell all.

He did tell. A simple story. As his even voice related it, it began with a phone call from William in New York. He'd just heard that a woman he knew long ago was in bad shape, the kind of thing that required a lot of nursing and individualized care, and he'd like to help out. If he sent Cyrus a check, would he attend to the details and turn the money over in any way he thought feasible?

She did look up now. Jefferson Memorial, could that be what the building was? No, not possible, was she getting disoriented, how could it be the Jefferson Memorial in that direction?

"We talked at some length. We went into the tax aspects. I proposed a trust whereby he or some representative would be able to oversee the expenditures. I pointed out the hazards of giving money without making some provision for ascertaining how it was to be spent. He listened carefully—you know what an agreeable man—but his mind was made up. I was to give the money and say it was from an unknown donor, and that was to be that. An outright gift, with no strings attached."

"So you complied."

"Yes. I called one day and went around the next afternoon. It was a small house in Takoma Park, neat and clean but surely not ostentatious. The woman, Marcy, lived with her sister, and she was the one I spoke to. She was taken aback, shocked, I should say, but when she understood she said they could certainly put the money to good use—nursing care for a stroke victim was very expensive and they had no resources except a small annuity from their father and the salary she made teaching school."

"And that was the whole thing?" Her voice shook: interjecting herself despite her resolve.

"She asked me if I'd like to see the recipient. The sick woman, that is. But since I was not to tell her who the donor was, I didn't see the use. Besides, I'm not very good with sick people, I get queasy in hospitals." Mr. Depew gave a sheepish smile: human after all.

"And you never went back, made sure Marcy was getting any benefit from all that money?"

"I explained. Dr. Gardiner wanted no involvement. There were to be no conditions. I can add, however, that the sister seemed a responsible woman, truly concerned about Miss Drummond's welfare, I saw no reason to think—"

"Oh, responsible. I was there," she burst out. "I mean, I saw Marcy. There's no decent therapy, not even a trained nurse; for hours she lies there unattended."

Mr. Depew unfolded his hands and said Dr. Gardiner had been apprised of the risks. "I may add, Mrs. Gardiner, that this is a not uncommon problem. If you give money outright, you have no authority to direct its use in future. I have a client right now who embodies just such a dilemma. A year or so ago she donated a park in a run-down section of town, a pretty place with fountains, landscaping, outdoor furniture. Well, she called me in great distress last week. She'd driven by, and the park was a mess. Furniture stolen, flower beds vandalized, drug dealing, filth. I explained that since she hadn't made any provision for upkeep, she couldn't now take the position . . ." He was talking as if to make up for his previous reserve; maybe this was his way of saying, look, I'm not a robot.

Should she talk more herself, tell them the intimations of danger in regard to Marcy that grip her? No, because Victor was talking. "So now that you've found out in the first place that William did give money to this unfortunate woman, and in the second that he did so without any mechanism for imposing conditions, you can see that it would be foolhardy to make a further contribution. It would in effect be pouring money down an unsupervised and irresponsible drain."

She nodded. That cutting voice, the gaze that went over her, past her, with its air of disdainful judgment—what a fool she'd been. She'd thought it was concern for people, for *her* that impelled him to overrule his colleague. Nothing like it. It was simply concern for money. Never mind that the money in question belonged to someone he hated. Forget that he thought she'd gotten it by reprehensible means. Money, anyone's money, was important, a sacred object: that was the real code. And that was why he wanted her to know the facts: his reverence for her money was greater than his distaste for her.

As to telling him anything more, staying with him a second longer than was necessary—heaven forbid. It remained only to summon up a voice as disinterested as his, and express her insincere gratitude, and with dignity, thank goodness, intact, say goodbye and clear out fast.

Chapter
SEVENTEEN

A PHONE BOOTH WOULD SERVE THIS TIME; one in the lobby of the building. "Tad? It's Nan. I need your help."

She heard him tell someone he'd be with them in a second. Then he told her to ask away.

"Well, I've found the nurse William went with. The one who—oh, God, it's too complicated, I can't possibly go into it on the phone."

"Okay, we'll have lunch—no, wait. I have to speak at a lunch meeting."

"Tad, I could stop in at your—"

"Tell you what. I'll come to your place. Noon? Roughly noon—that sound all right? No, don't worry, work out fine for me."

A man knocked on the door of the booth, met her indignant stare, and slunk away. "Tad, I can't thank—"

"Don't try. Hang in there."

Ten o'clock now. Hang in for a couple of hours. More suspense, but this time she could stand it. It was not a discipline in uncertainty; she couldn't remotely link herself with those tortured souls waiting to find out was the biopsy negative, did they pass the exam, was their boy among the missing? In one sense there was no suspense at all because she knew in her heart Tad would agree; what she planned to ask was a commission to call on just those attributes of tact and expertise and affability he dispensed most freely. Look at the promptitude with which he wrangled for her those evaluations—no fuss, simply that expedient use of charm plus the certain knowledge of procedure. This would take more extensive knowledge, maybe a more calculated charm, but she was not in any doubt that he would say yes.

Back at the hotel, she looked around the living room that was turning out handy after all. She could make it presentable for him, at least: the unspeakable orange cushions hidden in the closet, the blinds raised to let in the thin November sun, the suitcase rack that she'd been using for old newspapers relegated to the bedroom. And fresh coffee, that first requisite, made in the small electric coffee maker that went into her suitcase ahead of bras and stockings. There was still the institutional look, a room designed for the careless depredations of the transient and the facile dabs of the help, but at least when Tad knocked on the door, natural light was casting gaudy lines across the green and tan rug, and the smell of coffee dimmed the innate smells of dust and polish and cigarette smoke. And he was carrying a bottle of wine wrapped in blue and silver paper which he handed her with a courtly bow—the morning transformed.

"Tad, how do you do it? A famous doctor, to get away on a moment's notice."

He put his papers on a table and said one of the perks of fame was the ability to be dictatorial about one's time. Then the pleasant gaze went over her. "Nan, let's have it."

Now she realized how she should have spent the morning. A stern ordering of the facts instead of that mindless puttering with decor; surely a busy doctor deserved that much. That confused and ambiguous story—where should she begin?

"Nan, take your time."

That was Tad: discerning. She took a breath and asked if he by any chance remembered a nurse called Marcy Drummond.

"Let me think."

"As I told you, William went out with her."

He assumed the look of rueful deprecation they all wore when this topic came up.

"Okay, I know what you're going to say; William went out with lots of girls. This one was special. You wrote her a letter," she added, as if this would clinch it.

"I did?"

"You said she should do nothing about whatever it was the two of you had talked about the day before."

"Marcy Drummond. Sure. I remember now. The two of us were friendly in the kidding, semi-hostile way a cocky resident and a bright nurse very often are friendly. But now, that letter . . ."

"I figured it was connected with her having had a breakdown."

"Right," Tad said. "For some reason she went to pieces, poor darling, and that letter must have been because in some way she muffed up, and I counseled her sitting tight, but it didn't help because if I remember right they fired her."

"It is right. And then she went downhill fast—oh, it was wretched—and three years ago, age forty-two or maybe -three, she had a stroke."

"Marcy Drummond, that little beauty, with a stroke— Jesus. What a thing." He got up and turned the wine bottle, so the bow on its gift wrapping showed. Then he asked how she knew all this.

She sighed and pointed out that she'd been down here almost a week.

"A very productive week," he said reflectively. "Especially if someone in the state you tell me Marcy's in lets you read her letters."

"She didn't let me. She's alone from two to four, between when an attendant leaves and her sister comes, and, well, I didn't ask."

"Nan, the detective." His voice was noncommital. No rebuke, but also no special commendation. Well, he was right. Whatever the circumstances, reading other people's mail was not among the more attractive measures. "But what I don't get," he went on, "is what you expect to find. Oh, I know it's your old theory, but in this case does it really hold water? Because a girl has an affair with a man and subsequently goes into a tailspin, why should you think the two must be connected?" Well, of course it troubled him. Tad also knew about the sour aftermath a casual affair could leave: if Gail didn't go into a tailspin herself after they broke up, surely that wretched boy of hers could be said to have suffered. But this was a piece of his past she hoped Tad never discovered that she knew about. She sat opposite him and spoke quietly. She said her reason for assuming that the connection between William and Marcy was a significant one was that he gave her money.

"He was a very generous man, your husband."

"Yes. I'm the first to know. But even the most generous man in the world doesn't turn over a couple of hundred thousand dollars to an old girlfriend he hasn't seen in twenty years unless something crucial went on somewhere along the line."

"Good God. Two hundred thousand. You sure of that?"

"Very sure."

"When was this?"

"Three years ago. Just after she had the stroke."

"Bowls you over, doesn't it?" A man getting his bearings,

he closed his eyes for a second and leaned back in the green armchair. Then he said, okay, William had a generous heart, self-evident. But it didn't follow that he also had reason for a guilty conscience. "Marcy's breakdown—maybe she just fell apart. It goes on more than we think. The difficult working conditions, plus the insufficient pay, plus of course the strains that come with the job—no wonder nurses go to pieces."

Wrong. It's the doctors who go to pieces. There was that study just the other day, didn't you read it, thirty-six percent of the doctors in some state or other on tranquilizers, seventeen percent hospitalized at some time for crackup. She didn't say it, but she had to exercise real control not to say it. How it always happens, she thought. Even with someone who's proved himself a dear friend, it happens. A single inapt word, and there you are back in the doctor-nurse relationship, feeling the old grievances, subject to the inescapable resentments.

What she said was that Marcy had been a solid character. Excellent record, lots of interests, friends. On the evidence, not a candidate for breakdown. "Tad, didn't William ever say anything about her?"

"You forget. In those days we weren't equals. A staff doctor may have lunch with a resident, he walks with him down the hall, asks for his assessment about the cases. But a heart-to-heart about his love life? Never."

The coffee was steaming; its smell permeated the room. She walked over to it, put her hand on the pot, but she didn't pour it. "Then it comes down to Marcy. Marcy's my only hope."

"And with a stroke she can't talk, is that the problem?" Tad asked.

"She could talk if I knew the questions to ask her. She could say yes or no. And I'm close to knowing. Okay, not really close, but I'm getting there, I feel sure of it, just a little more digging, or maybe, I don't know, a rearrangement of the clues I've dug up so far. Tad, I'm on the edge of something; look at all the progress I've made already."

Did she shock him with all this frenzied confidence? "It would help Marcy too," she went on more quietly. "Her sister treats her like a moron; that's inevitable, I guess, I even catch myself sometimes. But she isn't a moron; she has her old perceptions, I know she does; the intelligence is there behind those angry eyes. She might even get some relief. I mean, something traumatic she's carried around all these years. But" —she saw his watchful gaze—"her sister doesn't want her to talk. She won't let me see her. She says if I come again she'll call the police."

"Why should she be so vehement?"

"Well, first I didn't understand it either. But now that I know about the money, that kind of ban makes sense. Because she's not spending that windfall on Marcy, not remotely. She's salting it away for herself, and naturally she doesn't want a nosey visitor to get into position to find that out. She even fired someone, a woman Marcy cared for, because she got wind of William's gift, and she was smart enough, this Glady Johnson, to cotton to the truth."

"She must be spending some money. Full-time nursing, it can take a bite out of even two hundred thousand."

"But she doesn't have a full-time nurse, that's the point. She has a woman, not even a trained one, who's there from ten to two. That means Marcy's alone in the morning after her sister leaves and again for a couple of hours till Linda gets home at four. And if Linda goes out at night—I suppose sometimes she had to go out—more aloneness."

"Jesus. Someone paralyzed, alone in a house."

Well, of course he understands, he can appropriate the panic. "You know what? I wouldn't be surprised if Linda wants to kill her. Tad, don't look at me like that. I'm not saying she *will* kill her. I'm just thinking of the mixed feelings."

"You mean, she takes devoted care of the patient and resents having to take devoted care?"

More discernment—why is she surprised? Anyone who has dealt with this situation comes up against the ambivalence.

"It would be a pushover. Even—well, feeding her something harmful. Now I think of it, Linda went out of her way to mention Marcy's longing for cake and ice cream. Maybe she's not deliberately planning to raise the level of sugar in Marcy's blood, but the idea must be there, bouncing around in that aggrieved mind." There was a knock on the door—the maid for those blouses Mrs. Gardiner had wanted laundered, but she said forget it, some other time; yes, I changed my mind. "And when you think how easy," she said then. "A patient who has diabetes, well, stroke patients very often do develop diabetes, just slip those desserts on her tray a few days in a row—why am I telling you this, you probably wrote the book."

He nodded. He said he knew the damaging effect a four- or five-day supply of forbidden sweets could have on someone like Marcy.

"That Linda, she may have been a perfectly nice woman once, but now she's seething with animosity; she's hard and bitter—well, why wouldn't she be hard and bitter?"

Tad nodded and said he understood the problem, but the difficulties seemed to be built in and he wasn't sure what could be done about them.

"Well, I thought if she were in a nursing home, Marcy, I could talk to her then. There'd be nothing to keep me away except the standard restrictions. And her health would be monitored; she'd be safe."

He looked up: that ingenuous smile. "Is that where I come in? I'm to get this woman into a nursing home?"

She nodded; that was where he came in.

Tad spoke slowly. "If the sister won't pay for adequate care at home, she surely won't shell out for a nursing home. Those places cost the earth. Especially the kind that take in the totally disabled."

"But Tad, I'm going to pay, me, it's what I told them this —I mean, it'll be on me. My money." That shrillness is her voice. She's a taciturn girl, basically. Someone who *listens*. She never talks this much, never. Between this morning's interview with Mr. Depew and this talk with Tad, she figures she's expended more words than she usually lets loose in a month. Her quota, and she hasn't finished yet.

She said she couldn't swing the nursing home on her own—Marcy would never agree. Especially since she was dead set against hospitals, wouldn't set foot in one. But if Tad would get in the act. A doctor. Someone who knew Marcy long ago, must have had a friendly relationship with her. "Oh, Tad, you can charm anyone," she wound up.

He didn't protest the description. He just said it wouldn't be easy. But he did happen to know a place. In Maryland, north of College Park. Not much to look at, old Victorian buildings and scrawny lawns, but expert care, he knew for a fact. And since he'd done some work with the director—"Nan, don't get your hopes up. These places have waiting lists a mile long. But with some clout—hey, is that coffee over there? Sit down and I'll bring it to you. No, I insist. Doctor's orders. All these obstacles, a woman who can't talk, a sister who might want to kill her—you poor child, what nightmares you must have."

She stood a second next to the end table. Should she offer to open the wine he brought? No, he was right; at this juncture coffee was better. She moved the wine an inch, seeing the papers under it: Dr. Thadeus Collins, discoverer of the Edoac Treatment, will be guest speaker at a lunch meeting on Thursday, November 12.

November 12. Today. He was in big demand as a speaker, wasn't he, she said as she went back to the couch.

He handed her a cup. "I stay within the allotted time. I tell a joke at the beginning. I make a complimentary remark about the director's wife. Why shouldn't they want me?"

"Also, you did something memorable. Like discovering —that treatment, Edoac, what is it?"

"Not so memorable," he said. "Just a lot of mileage for a simple idea. Drink your coffee, you need it."

She did drink. She put her feet up and rested her head on a pillow and felt the tension drain away. A man who promised to take care of things; you might bridle at some of his male assumptions, but you welcomed the acquiescence to his peremptory commands. "All these conferences," she said dreamily. "Do they always meet here in Washington?"

"Not on your life. We doctors are too smart for that. Last year I got to Vienna once, Copenhagen once, Hawaii twice, New Orleans once."

"All on the house?"

"All on the house," he said. "Next year I'm hoping for Alaska."

She could see him, the pleasant gaze and easy smile set against a panorama of snow and glaciers. Or didn't they have glaciers in Alaska? In any case, always the same introduction: the distinguished Dr. Collins, who discovered the Edoac Treatment.

"I suppose corporate heads do better," he said, "dancing girls with their dinners, but after them we doctors—I thought I told you to sit down."

He did tell her, but there she was pacing again. Edoac. Simple word: five letters, three syllables. Or is it not simple; is there some inner meaning she's not getting? When she was in college, she took a course in poetry appreciation. Read it again, the professor would say. What's the poet telling us with that metaphor? Explicate, explicate! She never could. She could look over a page of chemistry and it was forever imprinted on her mind; she could glance at a string of dates and they slipped effortlessly into her store of mental notes, but explicate—never. For all her assiduous reading of the poems, something eluded her; she couldn't grasp that kernel of meaning the professor insisted was there. You tell us, she wanted to call out to him in class. You explicate, she wished to shout, but of course she couldn't.

Neither could she ask Tad to explicate Edoac. Or rather she did ask and he didn't answer. Curious. Medical terms are usually more complex. They go in for multiple syllables; they flaunt prefixes and suffixes like *chloro* and *ozene* that are designed to sound abstruse and evoke awe. Edoac, on the contrary, is pared down almost to the point of childishness. Forthright, breezy. Like Tad. Edoac. And why the vowel first? Why not a strong letter to start, like the D?

She pulled aside the blind. No memorable buildings visible here, just rows of apartment houses, a garage, a supermarket. The Washington where people live. Real people. They hustle to move up on the civil service ladder; they do elaborate computations of carryover leave; they know someone who knows someone who knows the new administrator. In Washington, we're all acronyms.

"Nan, you okay?"

"Oh, sure." An acronym, that would explain that prefatory E. A letter with a function, but what? All this tussling with a little word is numbing her. Fine, she told Tad, but she's not; she's exhausted, smitten with the sudden desire to lie down on the practical orange and green fabric with which Sherbourne Arms covers its couches. This overwhelming languor—is it the strain of all this talking? Or is it just because she got up so early this morning? Early! E for Early, how's that? EDOAC. Early Something of Something Something.

And she knows! That professor was right; there is a kernel of meaning—it comes to her as she hears Tad ask what's so interesting outside the window. Superimposed on the apartments across the street, she sees the crumpled pages that had been tucked into the evaluation folders, and the scribbled words in William's undoctorlike handwriting, and she knows everything. No, not quite. She simply knows that the connection between the meaning of Edoac and every other fact she's painstakingly acquired over the past five days would be significant, would alter her most basic conclusions, if she had time to figure it out.

She doesn't have time. She's impelled by two purposes. She has to get Tad out of here before she falls asleep, and she has to keep him from suspecting that it's her aim to get him out. Two actions that contradict each other. Impossible. Maybe if she were alert, possessed of all her resources, she could work out that paradoxical chore. She is not alert; her head is wobbling; she longs for sleep with all the fierceness of her suddenly addicted being.

"Nan, anything wrong?"

Ho, ho, he's making jokes. My friend the executioner is a wit. "Why should there be?"

"You look so—maybe you want more coffee."

The coffee. Ha! That was it. She looked blankly past him. Keep walking. Don't stop for a second: prescription for survival. The patient, who is herself, is enjoined to perpetual mobility by the nurse, who is also herself.

He, on the other hand, settled himself in his chair with an air of preparing to wait it out. "Your lunch meeting," she said.

"What about it?"

"Don't you have to get there?"

"I'm not on till two o'clock."

"Program says one-thirty. I peeked." An attempt at a sickly smile.

"We know better than that, don't we? Those doctors, at one-thirty they'll still be at the roast beef and tiny peas." A man at his ease, he folded a languid arm behind his head.

She moved a sluggish leg. She could of course try to run past him. Stumble past the chair where he was sitting, and the couch where she kept imagining herself lying, and head, in her rocky state, for the door. But the man at his ease was watching her; any haphazard movement on her part would be met by a calculated one on his.

"What's the joke?" she said.

"What's that?"

"Your starting joke for today."

"Oh, I never settle on one in advance. I'll decide when I see how the audience shapes up."

Bully for him. A man with options. Whereas she can't think of even one simple device, one foolproof little contrivance to remove from her room a man who is determined to stay in it. And meanwhile that inner mandate tells her she has to keep moving, one leg, then, ponderously, the other leg, up and down on this ghastly green and tan rug.

"Did you drive here or come by taxi?" she said.

He said his car was parked in front; why does she ask?

"It's just"—make it good now—"your Washington traffic. Lord knows how you manage. Yesterday I saw a tie-up at the corner, no reason at all, just routine mess; one driver said he'd been there twenty minutes."

No score either way. He gave her a quizzical look—what she interpreted as a quizzical look—and said not to worry; he was an old hand at traffic messes.

She watched him watching her; the buckling legs, the heavy head. Whatever happens, she thought, at least I'll be asleep. There won't be any conscious suffering. Like the criminals executed by means of a kindly injection. But that's indecent, really; it's worse than anything—surely even the most miserable wretch deserves to be awake, fully participating, at the most momentous of all events.

If she didn't look at the couch, would that annul her longing to be on it? She stared at the picture above. A landscape. Standard hotel painting. Standard, but she knew that lake, she suddenly realized. Crazy. To have been here five days and not notice it until now. The double-L dock, the irregular conformation of land, the slanting roof, the strip of beach dissolving into the flurry of trees . . . it was the place, she could swear it, her father used to take them to every summer.

That lake was her childhood. There she mastered the beautiful peril of stepping from dock to rowboat. Someone asked her, Are you the one with the nifty crawl? She wouldn't get out of the water till dark because her new bathing suit was too tight. And now this man was proposing to end it—all those rich days on the lake gone for nothing.

Even if it wasn't her lake; it was a different one, now that she looked more closely. Different house, different angle between dock and beach. Didn't matter. He would curtail it unless she thought of something. Well, think! Men are tricked all the time into action they don't desire. By guile or astute persuasion, they're induced to strap bombs to their waist, dive into the hold of ships, renounce the woman they love, hand over the family property—surely it should be possible to get a man to leave a room where he's bent on staying. If she could sleep for fifteen minutes, she could think of it when she woke. If she slept for fifteen minutes, she wouldn't wake. Keep walking. Every maze has its exit, every quandary its solution.

"Do you really have to go to that lunch meeting?" she said.

"Why do you keep talking about my meeting?" A shade of irritation in his voice: the first she'd ever heard from him.

"Because . . . well, I have a tremendous favor. I have no right to ask, you being so busy and all." Her eyelids wouldn't stay up; she clutched at a table to dispel the blur. "Tad," she said, "I'm scared."

"Scared?" The arm that had been behind him uncurled to join the other on his lap.

"Of Victor. Terrified. I mean, he's coming here, he's due any minute"—another stumble; her legs were disinclined to obey orders from her brain—"he said twelve-thirty, but maybe a few minutes late."

"Victor coming here!" Tad was sitting straight.

"If I'd had my wits about me, I'd have said meet me someplace else."

"Victor coming here!" Second time he'd said it.

"He has it in for me; the way he feels, he might do anything," she said, and in her ears her voice sounded slurry, like Marcy's. "Terrible man. Scary. So if you were here, in the bedroom, listening—Tad, is it too much to ask?"

He was standing. "Victor coming!" Was he really saying it a third time?

"Tad, don't go to that meeting; please stay here, I beg you."

She saw his gaze take in the two doors. Door to the hall, connecting door to the bedroom. Still a man with options.

"Would you do it? Wait in there? Just to make sure I'm all right? Tad, would you?"

His feet did a little shuffle. He moved to the connecting door, then back to the table to pick up his papers, then a pause that seemed to her interminable—how long was she expected to remain upright while the man with options made up his mind—then the door to the bedroom again.

"Tad, swear you'll stay there. Swear it."

Light from the window shone on the sandy hair and suddenly distorted face. "Okay," he said, as he put a hand on the doorknob. "Yes," as he opened it and walked in.

So he was in there. In the room with the magazines piled on the night table for when she couldn't sleep, and the stockings that had a run so she left them on the floor, and the lipstick that turned out to be the wrong color after she bought it at the drugstore yesterday, and the blouses to be laundered, only she told the maid to come back—she could see him in that scene of private clutter. But she couldn't see anything else. Was he standing there alert, one who had seen through her ploy and was just biding his time till she'd have stumbled to the couch and succumbed to sleep? Or was he heading out fast, past the neglected blouses and ineffectual magazines, because if Victor was coming, his plans had best be altered?

Which? If she could make it to the keyhole, she might have an inkling, but she couldn't make it to the keyhole; she couldn't move; she might not even have the strength to pick up the phone.

"Hilton Hotel," she told the switchboard. "Yes, I know it's in the book, but I broke my glasses." The chair wasn't where she expected it to be; she slid down the wall to the floor. "Hilton? Mr. Hemmings, please. Victor Hemmings. No, I don't know his room number—listen, it's an emergency."

Hundreds of people calling there every minute. If they want to cancel the date for cocktails, or change tomorrow's lunch, or ask if Row J Center is okay for the ballet, Emergency is what they say; operators know better than to pay attention. Besides, why his hotel? Why not the law office, where he was three hours ago? Well, she knew why. Because the name and number of the law office were in her pocketbook across the room, and she hadn't the strength to get there. It was the Hilton or nothing. Anyhow, lunch time, he wouldn't be there; why in the world should he be there?

"Hello?" That noncommital voice.

"Victor? It's Nan Gardiner."

"Who?" Of course he doesn't believe it, that slurred voice that sounds like no one he's ever known, and even if he does believe, why should he want to hear what she has to say?

"Could you come over right away, please, now, this minute . . ."

"Nan?"

"Listen, I . . . I think . . ." she said into the phone which she then dropped, which she couldn't pick up, which was too heavy to be picked up even though she heard his voice issuing from it. Why, When, Where, How, he must be saying, all the reasonable queries a man puts when a hysterical voice comes at him out of the blue. Especially Where. She'd neglected to tell him the name of her hotel; that pertinent fact escaped her, and without calling every hotel in Washington, which could take forever, there was no way he could find out. She made a try at the receiver again, but it weighed a ton; she couldn't lift it; she could only lie there, passing out ignominiously on the green rug so that all her cleverness would have gone for nothing.

Chapter
EIGHTEEN

A LOT OF PEOPLE ARE TALKING at once. Hold her up, they say. Keep her moving, they shout. I'll take this arm, they boisterously affirm. She opened her eyes. Not a lot of people, just two, Victor and another man whose buck teeth and sloping forehead looked vaguely familiar.

She closed her eyes. She is still walking up and down on the green and tan rug, and Tad is watching from his chair, all smiling and complacent because he knows she won't be able to keep going; eventually she'll crumple and lie down, and then with the neatness and calm dispatch that is his trademark, he'll be free to do whatever it is he plans to do.

"She's okay," Victor said. "Just she has to walk it off."

She shook her head; things cleared a little. What happened? she meant to say, but it came out a gurgle.

"Little more," Victor said. "Few more steps."

"Upsadaisy," the man said through earnest buck teeth.

"Doing fine," Victor said.

"Maybe a little coffee," the man said as they mercifully eased her into a chair at last.

Coffee? Something about coffee? "No," she cried, but Victor pushed her back down. It was all right, he said—he sent the other out to be tested; just a few sleeping pills is what he thinks—this is a new supply; restaurant just sent it in.

"Drink up," said the man, who was the relief desk man, she now saw, the one who yesterday explained the mechanics of sending out laundry.

The coffee was strong and hot; she drank, asked for more, closed her eyes again, understood from the frenzied motions of the two men that this was their signal to hoist her up, opened her eyes.

"Guess she just got blue," the man said.

"I guess so," Victor answered.

"I see it all the time. Young girl trying to make out on her own, after a while it gets to her. No job, no friends, money running out—this can be a cruel city."

"I'm sure it is," Victor said.

"Sometimes we find them in time, sometimes we don't. Well, they shouldn't have those sleeping pills so easy to get hold of."

"I guess not," Victor agreed.

"You'll stick around, now you're here? Make sure she's okay? The management doesn't want trouble."

Victor said he'd stick around, which emboldened the man to put on the coat of his uniform and say call if you need anything and go out.

She sat silent, taking in the room. The utilitarian furniture, the evocative painting, the blinds through which sun was filtering. Imagine, sun, as if it were any ordinary day. She turned to Victor and said she wasn't blue. That is, she wasn't depressed. That is, she had not tried to kill herself with sleeping pills.

Victor sat with his noncommittal face.

"You don't believe me."

"I guess you've had a rocky time," he judicially said.

"Listen. Things aren't what you think. See that wine? He brought it. He was going to use that, but I had the coffee made, that was more convenient." Hopeless. She has never been able to convince him of anything, why should she expect it to change now? How do you feel? was all he said.

Well, why complain; come to think of it, it's the kindest thing he's ever said to her, the least charged with animosity. How does she feel? Actually, as if she'd like an indefinite continuance of this languid arrangement, she in this chair, Victor in another, while the sun makes mottled patterns on the furniture, and she knows there is no urgency; he's held his misconceptions this long, whatever explanations are due can be put off to some more accessible time.

In fact, she was the one who would like an explanation. How did he get here? she said.

"Jumped into a cab," he began, but she shook her head. That dumb phone call. She hadn't told him where she was staying.

"Right. But, well, I knew already." And when she sat silent, "The police told me," he went on. "They, um, asked if I knew anything about your accident. Driving without brake fluid, is that what happened?"

Oh, God. His tone held no reproach, but he must know that if she gave his name to the police in connection with that accident, it was because she considered him capable of having caused it: There's this lawyer who has it in for me. So they had gone to his hotel, two of Washington's finest, or maybe to the office where he was busy with a client; they had burst in and asked if he took brake fluid out of a car in the parking lot of the Sherbourne Arms, and he had been under the compulsion of explaining that no, he didn't.

Of course he didn't. She knew who did.

"I'm sorry. I hope they—"

"Good thing they came," he said. "Otherwise I wouldn't have known where to find you."

Indisputable. But the matter was not finished; something nagged at her that it wasn't. Victor didn't meddle with her brakes, she knew who did, who must have. . . . He'd tried twice now. Three flops and you're out—the gentlemanly routine. But this man was not a gentleman; his determination was too strong for that. Having failed in two attempts he was not going to let it ride, he couldn't; he'd simply go at it from another direction.

She sat straight: languor not permissible after all. "What time is it?"

"Quarter of two."

"He's going to get Marcy. Oh, listen, I can't explain. Just come, we have to—"

Victor sat unmoving. As if any of this were susceptible to lucidity, his lucid voice pointed out that an hour had passed since her phone call to him, ample time for this He, whoever he was, to get Marcy, whatever that meant. Besides, she, Nan, should be taking it easy, shock to her system, sensible health measure, still not fully recovered, and so on.

"But he couldn't until now, don't you see; the attendant is there till two—the irony is I'm the one who told him. So he's just waiting till Marcy's alone, I mean, if he didn't get me he has to get her, she's the only one who—Please come. Please. I'm not demented, really I'm not, I'll explain on the way."

But she didn't. As it worked out, once he had acquiesced and helped her downstairs and got a taxi, he did the talking. In response to her shrill exhortations about haste and danger, he told the driver to step on it, and then he leaned back and talked.

"Nan, I guess you know something about the business of getting to be a doctor. That ordeal—I don't mean just the grueling work. But there's the standard of excellence—the pressure never lets up. You drive yourself in high school so you'll get into college, and you keep pushing in college so you'll make med school, and in medical school you know you have to shape up if you want a good internship—well, it goes on in other professions too, but it's worse, everyone agrees, in medicine, because it's paired with killing hours and inhuman schedules. Relentless—why do you look like that?"

She looked like that because of his tone. Portentous and defensive at once.

"Okay, so it takes its toll. I don't know if you know; they try to keep it quiet, but doctors do crack up. A big, blazing breakdown that takes them out of commission for maybe —Ah. So you do know. Or it can be quieter. Years and years of meeting the mark, and then inside something snaps. Maybe a mistake in judgment. A moral lapse. The normal ethical precepts for a brief time suspended. What I'm trying to say is it all adds up, the hustling to stay on top, and the sleepless nights, and the brutal work, and the sacrifices of others—don't forget those because the doctor never does; it's always in their weighing on him that to get him where he is some wife or sister or mother took it on the chin, it all comes together—"

"Why are you telling me this?" She sat on the edge of her seat. There was a Please Do Not Smoke sign, but the taxi smelled of cigar smoke.

"Because it's the only way to make clear—"

"Victor. Please. Just tell it straight."

"Well, twenty-one years ago—Why are you shaking?"

"Go on."

"In that year, William had a patient with a terminal illness. No question. She was going to die. Lung cancer with complications: the best medical opinion gave her six months, seven at the outside. However, it was very much in the interest of her husband, who happened to be a senator assigned to the Armed Services Committee, that she not linger for her full six months. The woman he was planning to marry wouldn't wait. Or he was afraid she wouldn't wait. As things turned out, she didn't have to wait. The wife died after six weeks, and he got his woman." The flat voice stopped while the driver maneuvered into a faster lane.

"All right, that's one side of it. The other side is that shortly after this let's say premature death, the small business William's sister and husband owned fell heir to a hefty defense contract. They'd been turning out radio amplifiers, strictly a two-bit operation, and all of a sudden they were in the big time, producing some part of the communication system for ships."

"Look. Just because—"

"It was strictly the senator's doing." he said. "Some very heavy footwork was needed to get a government contract for a small-time outfit like that, and he did it."

She braced her hands on the cracked leather seats. "Whatever you're trying to say, I don't believe it. No way. None of this proves anything. It's wholly circumstantial."

"Wholly," Victor said, and she saw how gaunt his face was. "But William once told me that twenty-one years ago he'd done something, a terrible mistake, he'd be sorry for all his life. We were on the beach; it was dusk, that hour when intimacy seems to seep in along with the darkness, and I said he was a saint, and he said, Oh, Christ, are you ever wrong, and then he told me . . . well, what I just said."

So I made a mistake—okay, I admit. She looked out at the nondescript streets. One of those sections of Washington that tourists have no reason to visit, a section they drive through only when it is necessary to get to someplace else. "If this is what you thought, why didn't you tell me when—"

"When he died? When you came to my office that time?"

Out of the corner of her eye, she could see him kneading his hands. "At first I didn't remember. It's not the kind of thing you want to remember about someone you care for. I really thought that you—well, you know. But after you blew your top, that outraged and sincere-sounding defense, something clicked. A mistake, a mistake he had mentioned in a suicide note—I thought, well, it's just possible . . ."

That sound must be her own breath being exhaled.

"That's why I came to Washington. To check the possibility out," he said heavily.

Ah. So he'd been here for the same reason she had. Victor, the detective, going after another aspect of William's past. "You could at least have told me this morning."

"I really couldn't. First, I wasn't a hundred percent sure. I had an appointment right after you left with a man who'd been a key aide on that committee; it was his testimony that clinched it. And also, I damn well wasn't going to say anything discreditable about William in front of that other lawyer. And besides—"

"Besides, what?"

"Nothing really."

She nodded. What he meant, what he couldn't say, was that standing with her unconciliatory look and combative manner this morning, Mrs. Gardiner had not exactly made herself a natural recipient for confidences.

"That's why he would never see his sister," she said. "He said she wouldn't want to come to the wedding, but she would have, of course; it was just that the sight of her must have made him so acutely miserable, she reminded him of everything he had to forget."

Then she heard what she'd said. She felt him look quickly at her and then look away. All right, so she did believe. She believed because it was the only thing that made it all hang together. As she'd said to Tad, a rearrangement of the clues. And holding tight to that bitter and ineradicable belief, she knew it was even more imperative to get to Marcy fast.

"Why are we stopped?"

"There's a red light."

Too cruel for the life of a woman to be dependent on the traffic pattern of midday Washington. If we make this red light. If that bus ahead pulls over to the curb. The smart thing would be to call someone. A family must live above them; why didn't she note the name as she fumbled with the door? Or there were people up and down the block—she closed her eyes, and memory gave her the image of a gray-haired woman on a porch across the street. She must know about Marcy; all the neighbors do, Linda regales them with stories: Tired, but I went out of my way to get this special bread she likes. Surely any of them would jump to help if there were some way to alert them. Ludicrous. We communicate with men traveling in orbit around the earth, but there is no mechanism for sending a message from a taxi on Nebraska Avenue to a woman sitting behind the bare branches of her wisteria in Takoma Park.

"Isn't there some other street?"

"Be even slower." But he tapped on the glass. "Listen, buddy, if we get a ticket, I'll take care of it."

"Funny. She can't talk now, but she couldn't talk then either."

"What's that?" Victor turned.

"Marcy. I mean, no one she could tell. Except she did tell someone, and he—Aren't we there yet?"

"Few more blocks."

"What time is it?"

"Just sit back."

Nonsense. Doesn't he know that if she sits back, what she sees is a zealous and loving nurse slipping into a room where she isn't expected and isn't seen, where she will forever wish she hadn't gone. . . . "Why can't he get ahead of that car?"

"He's trying, look how he—"

"Did you tell him it's life and death?"

"Nan, he's going as fast as he can."

Perhaps just the opposite, he's pretending to go fast while taking out on them his anger at the passenger who smoked despite the express mandate of that hand-printed sign. Or perhaps his last fare didn't give a tip, and for that oversight this fare must pay.

Anyhow, no one goes as fast as he can on the basis of someone else's anxiety. True, he's passed all trucks, he honked wildly to keep a car from coming out of a driveway, he performed a daring maneuver to switch lanes, but still he's within the bounds of acceptable driving. He doesn't cut out on a sidewalk, for instance, or crash through the window of a supermarket, or career past the policeman holding up traffic, and why should he? Dominic Forlini, how should he realize it's urgent enough to be worth ruining his taxi, losing his license, landing in jail?

Even Victor. He must think he's doing *his* best, communing up there with the driver, egging him on, but Marcy doesn't in fact exist for him either. He's taken her on faith. He surely can't imagine what it's like for a woman to lie helpless, trapped in speechlessness, while the embodiment of her worst fears materializes beside her. Lying alone all those hours, does she project a shape, a set of features, for her putative intruder? Is horror worse when it emerges with fidelity from nightmare?

"*What time is it?*"

"Quarter past."

Maybe that attendant stayed later today. Maybe Marcy groaned and pointed to her stomach; out of some prescient sense of foreboding she pretended she had a pain, and the woman with rare indulgence fixed some tea and waited while her patient drank it; she was still there consoling the sufferer. On the other hand, maybe it was ten minutes early when she untied the towel from around her waist, changed out of the rundown slippers, sent her You be a good girl now carelessly down the hall.

"Nan, which house?"

Mr. Forlini must have caught the urgency after all; he drove past it even as she called out to him to stop. The house looked as it always had. Silent, uneventful, a rebuke to those who claim houses are a reflection of the sensibilities of their owners. Linda's azalea bushes waved leggy spears of exactly the same length as did her neighbor's on the left; her porch flaunted the same chilled plants and overturned chairs as the one on the right. Maybe this wasn't even the right house; in her panic how would she know? But when she ran up, the bottom step that squeaked last time she set foot on it again made its small remonstrative noise; the bell sent back from that inner hall a familiar deadened ping.

A ping that no one answered. "Oh, God, we have to get in."

Victor had sized it up; he was already back down the steps, rummaging in that untended plot of ground. When he straightened, he had a medium-sized rock in each hand. "Which window, do you think?"

"This one. That. I don't know."

"Get out of the way, it might spatter—no, further back."

What a sight! A man with a gray herringbone suit, blue oxfort shirt, blue tie, preparing to hurl a rock through a window. "No, wait, you'll be hurt."

"Yes, wait," Tad said as he opened the door.

Chapter
NINETEEN

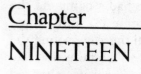

LIKE ANY HOST WHO FINDS himself confronting unexpected guests, Tad stood with reserved cordiality at the door. "This is a switch," he said.

Did he mean the fact of her and Victor being together? Victor holding a rock? Her having turned up here? One of them? All of them?

"Why the rock?" he quietly asked.

In the same tone of grim reasonableness, Victor said they hadn't known anyone was here.

"How come you *are* here?" she asked.

"You were the one. You asked me to come."

She could talk to him, but she couldn't look at him; there was no way she could force herself to exchange a direct glance with him. "*I* asked you?"

"Don't you remember—talk Marcy into the nursing home? So I went to my meeting, zipped through my speech, and I figured, why not now? But I got here too late," he added with the somber deprecation that forestalled her next question. "Thing is, poor girl, she's dead."

Nan felt her face stiffen into rigidity. I knew it, she thought. You go through the motions of those split-second dashes, so stylish, with cars usurping the road and people uttering their anguished exhortations and staid men getting into melodramatic postures: fair maiden snatched from the jaws of death—who doesn't cling to the myth? But in the end it's all meretricious; it's fun and games; nothing can stop what's been ordained.

Tad was still talking. Dead when he got here, he said with the same self-deprecatory shrug, and stepped aside so they could come in.

She could feel Victor standing back to give her the lead, and Tad coming after him. A dutiful procession, they come into the room with the wheelchair, the tray, the faded bathrobe, the steamy air of invalidism, and stand silent around the bed to pay the last respects to Marcy, who is certainly dead.

Not a serene death. A saga of violent suffering in the wide-open eyes, the bluish lips, the disarranged hair, the left hand clutching, as if in turmoil, at the blanket. "Must have been a second stroke," Tad said. "Maybe a rupture from an arteriosclerotic blood vessel, or maybe just an intense coughing fit that caused a cerebral infarction." And when they said nothing, "She may not have been having regular check-ups; with x-ray examination of the blood vessels they can sometimes catch that kind of susceptibility." Still silence. "At least if someone had been here to turn her head so the fluids could drain out," he said as he went to the door. "Well, I was just going to call the police when I heard you; I'll do it now."

Nan stood beside the pillow. "She was beautiful," she told Victor. "You can't tell now; it's cruel to look at her, but twenty years ago she was a beauty. A stunner, that's what everyone said. Well, maybe you can tell a little. The bone structure, see how good it is, and the eyes, and the whole shape of the face."

"Nan, I'm sorry. . . ."

"People loved her. Not just William. A man who wanted her to move with him to Carson City, and Pete, and Al, and someone called E, and I forget. And her patients. Most of all her patients. She was a good nurse, a wonderful one. With her talents, she could have gone in any direction. Art history. Clinical psychology—anything. But she wanted to be a nurse; that was what brought out the best in her; she couldn't imagine being anything else—Want to know how I know all this?"

"I think I do know," Victor said.

Well, maybe he did. Marcy, her twin, her double; maybe even in this sickroom, a hint of that affinity came through. Maybe he even knew the rest of it, that in a sense it was all her fault, because if she had let Tad pursue his course of an hour ago, Marcy would now be alive; there would have been no need for her to have died. Or put it another way. Marcy is lying with bluish lips and staring eyes because she, Nan, happened to think of a crafty way to get Tad out of her living room. One of us had to die. One. But surely that's not fair, it's carrying an affinity too far, for a single fate to be available for two women.

A dribble of moisture ran down from the corner of the distended mouth. She'd like to perform some gesture, fold the clawlike hand under the other one, or pick the bathrobe up from the floor, or comb back the hair as she once did in front of a mirror to reveal the lovely high forehead, anything to effect a little orderliness and grace. But when she stretched out her own hand, she didn't need Victor to remind her that it was best not to touch anything. From the next room they could hear Tad's voice. "Collins, right. Two l's. Oh, no question, I'm a physician, I'm very sure. Yes, of course I'll wait."

She spoke softly. "It wasn't a second stroke. I'm positive. At least—"

Victor nodded and touched her shoulder and led her out of the room.

"Police will be here in a few minutes," Tad said when they went into the living room. He walked over to the wing chair, and Victor positioned himself at one end of the couch, and this left her where she had been before, which was the desk chair. Were they really going to sit like this, the three of them facing each other in specious calm, for the eternity of a police department's few minutes? She rested her hand on the desk. All the papers gone: the valentines, the proposal from Lester, the condolence notes, the commendation from nursing school, the clipping about Miss Benjamin Franklin High School—did Linda allow herself a nostalgic reading before putting them back into that bottom dresser drawer? If you come again I'll call the police, Linda had told her, and she did come again, and the police were on their way. Crazy.

The police were on their way, and it occurred to her that this was the second time she and Tad had waited for them together, the two of them deep in their respective thoughts while in an adjoining room a dead body lay waiting for inspection on a bed. Life imitating life. Except there were differences; there were some salient and remarkable differences between that occasion and this.

"That note," she said, and it was obvious from the involuntary nod of Tad's head that he had gone back to that other time too; he knew exactly what note she was talking about. Well, he always was able to connect with her thoughts.

"I remember now. You went in while I waited at the door. Stand back, you said. Stay there, you told me. I was stunned, seeing William like that. I'd have obeyed anything. Then you gave me the note on a torn piece of paper. I did think for a second, not like William, so fastidious, he wouldn't have written his suicide note on torn paper. You tore it, didn't you? Did it say, Dear Tad? Or just Tad with a dash, like he sometimes wrote. That's it, I think. *Tad—So I made a mistake—I admit.*"

"It's an interesting theory," Tad said, and inclined his head.

"So I made a mistake—we all took for granted it was me, my marriage. But if that heading hadn't been torn off, it all would've looked different. Another meaning entirely."

Tad crossed his legs and said nothing.

"That mistake. Did he add potassium to that woman's intravenous—that would have been the obvious way. Or was it morphine? Or maybe digoxin? She could have been on any of them, the smallest increase would send her over."

"It's your story," Tad said.

"It isn't really," she said. "It's William's. William's and Marcy's. Because she saw him at it, she must have. Or somehow found out. Her beloved doctor, her hero. No, not just a doctor, a god. Someone who incarnated, he really did, the qualities of godliness. No wonder she was shattered. A god having a moral deficiency, committing murder."

"Are you really ready to assign that kind of act to your husband?"

She looked over at Victor; his reflective gaze met hers. Your decision, it despairingly said. Your problem.

"It's him or me," she said. "Yes, I'm ready to say that once he made a horrendous mistake, William did; he suffered a moral lapse."

Tad's lips curled. With complacence? With secret anxiety?

"But not as big a lapse as the man who hounded him." Footsteps on the porch, but not the police. The postman, maybe. Or a child running to retrieve a ball. "Poor, trusting Marcy," she said. "Out of the whole hospital, to confide in the one person who would listen to her story and decide to turn it to his own advantage. That's why you told her to do nothing, isn't it? You were going to do everything. Coast on it for the rest of your life. Starting with an unfavorable evaluation you could make him change." She pushed back the chair. A few minutes, did they say? Not long enough, she suddenly thought. Let them procrastinate, those summoned policemen, dawdle endlessly at the precinct house, stop first to see about an improperly parked car—it's all coming together; what she needs is time to fit in all the pieces.

"No wonder that evaluation wasn't in the files. An acquisitive nature—you stole Gail from him, didn't you; maybe you were getting ready to steal Marcy. That surefire technique, after all. Nurses do the dirty work. Nurses can't climb up in the scale. Nurses are second-rate people. It's very good," she said.

"Very good for us dumb-bunny nurses," she amended slowly. "God, how we fall for it," she said, and stopped. She was falling for it now. Or rather, she was replaying those moments in the cafeteria. The seductive warmth creeping up as a doctor with a persuasive voice and a round affable face says the things you always wanted to hear, that paean to your undervalued talents that is sweeter than any love song, that is, in effect, a love song—oh, it was disgusting, it was shameful, but the truth was, right now while she knew the full extent of his vileness, she still was conscious of the tug of that appeal.

"William saw right through you," she said harshly. "Leave it to William; it was his intention to keep you out of any decent hospital." Out of the corner of her eye, she saw Victor studying Tad with the fixed concentration of a watchmaker, a man at a microscope. "So that was bonanza number one," she said. "Your profit from William's terrible misstep. Forcing him to write you a new evaluation. But the second was bigger," she said, and leaned her elbow on the scarred surface of Linda's desk. "The second—dear God, when I think of it—to force William to turn over to you the idea that he was testing, he'd banked his soul on. EDOAC. Early Dose of Anti-Coagulant, that intuitive and wise and eminently simple idea, and it worked, think of it, it must have worked because Dr. Collins has been getting mileage from it all these years. Oh, William," she burst out, "you really paid for that mistake."

"Are you through?" Tad said.

"No, because you weren't. I guess William thought you were. He thought after twenty years he'd done enough penance; he could chance the joy of getting married, the time was finally—what word did he use?—propitious. Imagine. He was foolish enough to think that, my dear William. He'd be safe. Home free. He really took for granted blackmail has its own statute of limitations."

She was walking up and down, over to the china closet where a set of green and gold dishes sat under glass, back to the door, within inches of those aggressively decorated dishes again. "Even when you turned up at the wedding party, I think he thought it would be all right; we could have our happiness; after all why would you want to break it up? Well, I know why. Malice. Pure malice, that's all. Because there was nothing in it for you, nothing, I'd never have . . ." She could look at him; now that she'd got it all in order she could look him square in the face. "When did he know it was over, there was no use fighting? When you preempted the dinner for Ed Davis and he had to make up that story about having gout? No, I guess it wasn't till the trip to Aunt Martha's. You must have been in his office when I called. Quick thinking. I'll take her, you told him. Make up a meeting, you said. I guess by then he realized the truth; it would always be there, that moral failure, hanging over him; he'd never get out from under. Even though he knew I loved him"—no, she could not cry; now was definitely not the time to cry— "one way or other, you'd louse it up."

Her voice sank. Not a sound here in Linda's living room. Then Tad said it was all very ingenious and fascinating, but she didn't have a shred of proof.

Was that true? Surely the manner of Marcy's death must remain uncertain. I'm positive, she had said to Victor, but she wasn't; a pillow pressed on that helpless face until the legs stopped their futile thrashing and the single good hand slowly quieted would have caused the loss of oxygen to the brain that results in death, but so, incontrovertibly, would the aneurysm that Tad correctly described as being capable of causing a second stroke.

And probably no proof either of the attack on her; no use throwing out the accusation that after she found William's notes in the evaluation folder, after Tad saw her find them, he had gone to the motel parking lot and tampered with her brakes—his face would simply wear the look of practiced vacuity it was wearing now. But it was then, of course, that he had realized she was a threat rather than a plaything. Funny. She had thought it was a matter of a man no longer finding her attractive, the sexual element washing out, when it was simply the necessity for extermination slipping in.

For a second she thought of those notes. Did William accidentally let them fall into that folder—notes that were no longer any earthly use to him? But we're taught nothing is an accident, aren't we? Maybe in one of those abstracted moments when his right hand was doing something else, his left hand had casually dropped them in a file where it was just possible that some day, someone would have reason to look. His own private time capsule. "Those notes," she said to Tad. "Early dose of anti-coagulant. The idea put down in William's handwriting—they could prove something."

Tad made a gesture of impatience. Facile dismissal. But all he said, as he moved to the door, was that he'd wait for the police outside in his car.

"Listen. Don't think you can—" her bellicose voice began, but Victor's hand was on her arm. That quietly purposeful pressure that says Come on, or Stay back, or Let's go, or Hold it.

She held it, and the door closed on Tad's expressionless face. "Better this way," Victor said.

Better? What a word to use about a situation in which any direction down which one peered offered only the bleakest, the most overcast of vistas. Her pacing took her once more to the china cabinet, then she sat. Well, maybe for Linda it was going to be better; there was that. All that money. William's guilt money. For the past few years, Linda hadn't had much fun. She'd been cheating on Marcy, stashing away that windfall instead of using it on the sick care for which it was intended, but it was unarguable that for all her shabby tricks, she hadn't been having fun. Maybe now that she was rich and liberated and answerable to no one, she'd buy some clothes, try a new hairdo, develop a sweeter nature, get a whole new glowing personality. Money can do that. She might even turn out to resemble her sister. Instead of that primly defensive teacher, another Marcy.

"Nan, take my handkerchief."

"A young woman, faced with that responsibility," she said. "The only one who knew what the great Dr. Gardiner had done. Should she alert the hospital authorities? Should she go to the police? Should she pretend it had never happened? People twice as old as Marcy was then aren't able to handle that kind of dilemma, it destroys them. I mean, it was all on her, that intolerable burden. It was what she said, when she was having that breakdown no one could understand. All on me, she cried. All on me. But she had no one to advise her, no one even to talk to. No one, that is, but Dr. Collins, that cute resident, who told her to do nothing." She paused, but Victor didn't suggest that she should stop. "No wonder she would never set foot in a hospital again, nursing was out, visits to doctors were out; where was there anyone she could trust? I mean, Marcy, she was the real victim, the one whose life he took."

"It doesn't bear thinking of." How pale Victor was, his face some unlikely color of gray.

"And everything went against her, from the moment she found out. Irreversible. The indecision threw her, so she couldn't function as a nurse, and she got an abysmal job that led to a worse one, and then her health. Not being willing to see a doctor. People her age don't get strokes unless there's been some drastic neglect, something like blood pressure that's out of whack and doesn't get taken care of." Her throat ached from dryness. Some people— teachers, lawyers, singers—have work that keeps them using their voices all day long. How do they ever manage? "Even William's money couldn't help her. The way it didn't help his sister. True. That contract from the Navy, well, I understand, William wanted to make things up to her because of everything he'd got, but it didn't work like that; Jeanette was a lush by then, she'd married the man from dullsville, no way her life could head down a different track. Same with Marcy. The money did nothing, except in a way it made things worse; she lost the woman taking care of her, someone she really liked—oh, maybe it has to be like that. Guilt money. Maybe it's tainted, it has no power to do any good—do you suppose William figured that out?"

Victor was the one prowling now. His hand went out to

the glass door of the china closet, the wing chair, the desk, as if he'd just realized he was in a stranger's living room. "Think of something else," he said. "That treatment—what's its name? The anti-coagulant. Think of the lives saved by that."

"That's even harder. God, how wretched he must have been, unable to claim his own idea. You sensed it. You tried to tell me. Complicated depths, you said. The other side of good-time Charlie."

"If I'd known more I could have told you better—Listen. Wait here a second."

Wait why? But he moved quickly; he was at the door before she could say anything. Standing at the window, she saw him go down the steps, brush against one of the overgrown bushes, cross the street, and after a second's hesitation, move down the block a few yards to where a tan car was parked between two dark ones. His back was to her, she couldn't see his face. But she could see the dispirited slope of his shoulders as he put his hand on the door handle, jiggled it uselessly, and then walked around the car to the street side and did the same thing. Futile maneuver. Nothing gave. He stood there anyhow, next to that resolutely locked car, stood long enough so a laundry truck went by, and a stream of cars, and two boys on bikes. Then he slowly retraced his steps.

She was at the door when he came back. She'd never seen him like this, the sunken eyes, the heavy tread. "Done," he said. "Finished."

Was it always so hot in here, the stifling air to serve an invalid's unrelenting needs? "Victor . . . ?"

"He has a syringe. His hand is still clutching it. I sort of figured it when he walked out. At least, it was plain there was something he'd been planning to use on you, there must have been, otherwise why go to all that trouble to put you to sleep. He was going to wait till the sleeping pills worked, that surely was what he had in mind, and then he'd give you an injection to put you out for good, and then the syringe left in your hand as if you'd done it yourself. All very neat," Victor's neutral voice said. "It would have worked, no question. A nurse, after all, who knows about giving herself lethal injections, and also a demonstrably troubled young woman, someone the world holds in disrepute because of the circumstances of her husband's death . . ."

She saw the crease marks her fingers had left on Linda's curtain. "So now . . . you mean he used it on himself?"

Victor nodded. What he meant.

"He's there, in the car?"

"He's there. He locked himself in and—No, don't go. It's his decision. The only way for him, he knew it."

As it had been the only way for William, the consciousness of moral deficiency leading implacably to the plan for self-destruction. She stood beside the door. Should she run out? Nan, the nurse, trained in all those resuscitative tactics to be put at the service of the doomed, the dying. With that poker from the fireplace she could break through any car window. But Victor said no, Victor who was still standing with bent shoulders and shocked eyes, and there was such comfort in having someone else take over she suddenly felt as if she were floating, suspended above Linda's rug.

"Nan, listen to me. Those notes you were talking about —something William wrote down and then was blackmailed into giving up? And you have them, you somehow got hold of them? Well, it's proof all right. Tad knew it, he must have, otherwise he wouldn't be out there. You'll be able to put it together. Even without Marcy. Oh, won't be easy, not the pushover she'd have made it. But you can do it. A piece here, a piece there—you have yourself a case. Foolproof."

"You mean, bring out that whole miserable story! About William and that woman! Disgrace William's memory!"

"It's the only way to clear your own name. Get people to know the truth."

For a second she can't breathe. "*You* know it," she said.

"Oh, me. Right, I surely do. But just one person—you'll still be that woman in disrepute."

She looked out. Down the block, in a tan car, a man lay slumped behind the wheel. Dead tired, bystanders would think, if they happened to look in. "One person," she said slowly. "That's enough. . . . Oh, yes, I'm very sure. Positive. It's the way he would have wanted me to do it, my William."

Now the horns were beginning to blow. "Our William," Victor said.